KU-453-881

That kiss had been like nothing else she had ever known or could even imagine.

The very ground beneath her feet had swollen like the wave of a flooding river and burst, drowning her, and surely nothing could be the same again. It was as if she'd glimpsed the emotions only evoked by paint or charcoal on canvas.

Yet then he had vanished. Disappeared as if he was one of her dreams—half-hidden, desperately sought, but always elusive.

She closed her eyes for an instant and in that darkness she saw again the way he'd looked at her after they'd kissed. The sadness and longing, the burning fire of passion that had made her want nothing more than to leap into those flames and be completely consumed.

She knew she couldn't have been fooled by that glow in his eyes. There had been no artifice there in that instant—only raw, burning life.

Yet there had been that fathomless darkness, too. The darkness that had frightened her the first time she'd met him, when she'd seen the depths of anger he held deep inside himself. That had been there as well, fighting with the light of desire.

BETRAYED
BY HIS KISS

Amanda McCabe

MAGNA 25·02·15

First published in Great Britain 2014
by Mills & Boon, an imprint of Harlequin (UK) Limited,
Large Print edition 2015
Harlequin (UK) Limited, Eton House, 18-24 Paradise Road,
Richmond, Surrey TW9 1SR

© 2014 Ammanda McCabe

ISBN: 978-0-263-25530-0

Harlequin (UK) Limited's policy is to use papers that are natural,
renewable and recyclable products and made from wood grown in
sustainable forests. The logging and manufacturing processes conform
to the legal environmental regulations of the country of origin.

Printed and bound in Great Britain
by CPI Antony Rowe, Chippenham, Wiltshire

Amanda McCabe wrote her first romance at the age of sixteen—a vast epic, starring all her friends as the characters, written secretly during algebra class. She's never since used algebra, but her books have been nominated for many awards, including the RITA® Award, RT Reviewers' Choice Award, the Booksellers Best, the National Readers' Choice Award, and the Holt Medallion. She lives in Oklahoma, with a menagerie of two cats, a pug and a bossy miniature poodle, and loves dance classes, collecting cheesy travel souvenirs, and watching the Food Network—even though she doesn't cook.

Visit her at http://ammandamccabe.tripod.com and www.riskyregencies.blogspot.com

Previous novels by the same author:

TO CATCH A ROGUE*
TO DECEIVE A DUKE*
TO KISS A COUNT*
CHARLOTTE AND THE WICKED LORD
  (in *Regency Summer Scandals*)
A NOTORIOUS WOMAN†
A SINFUL ALLIANCE†
HIGH SEAS STOWAWAY†
THE WINTER QUEEN
  (in *Christmas Betrothals*)
THE SHY DUCHESS
  (linked to *Charlotte and the Wicked Lord*)
SNOWBOUND AND SEDUCED
  (in *Regency Christmas Proposals*)
THE TAMING OF THE ROGUE
A STRANGER AT CASTONBURY**
TARNISHED ROSE OF THE COURT
THE RUNAWAY COUNTESS††
RUNNING FROM SCANDAL††

And in Mills & Boon® Historical *Undone!* eBooks:

SHIPWRECKED AND SEDUCED†
TO BED A LIBERTINE
THE MAID'S LOVER
TO COURT, CAPTURE AND CONQUER
GIRL IN THE BEADED MASK
UNLACING THE LADY IN WAITING
ONE WICKED CHRISTMAS
AN IMPROPER DUCHESS
A VERY TUDOR CHRISTMAS
RUNNING INTO TEMPTATION††

*The Chase Muses
†linked by character
****Castonbury Park* Regency mini-series
††*Bancrofts of Barton Park*

DEDICATION

This book is for Kyle

'I love you with so *much* of *my heart*
that none is left to protest.'
—*Much Ado About Nothing*

Prologue

Tuscany—1474

The church was silent and marble-cold. Candles were lit over the altar, sparkling on the gilded image of the Virgin Mary surrounded by saints and solemn angels, but everything else was in darkness. Orlando Landucci was alone.

Except for the woman who lay on her lonely bier before the altar steps. His sister, gone from him now.

He knelt beside her, his hands clasped before him, but he could not pray. Even in this holy place he couldn't let go of the fierce anger burning inside of him.

Maria Lorenza's face, so delicately pretty in life, was pale and still. Her blond hair was hidden by the white linen wrappings and her brown eyes were closed for ever. A rosary was threaded through her cold fingers. Perhaps she was at peace now, at last. Her torment had been so great for so long. Yet how could she be, when her murderer was still out there?

Matteo Strozzi had not held the poison bottle to her lips, but he had surely guided her hand as she swallowed. The memory of his betrayal haunted even after all those months. The deep-dyed villain.

She wouldn't take Orlando's help before, but he would give it to her now. He owed it to her for the sisterly love she had long given him.

As he tucked a small bouquet of spring flowers into her hands with the rosary, he remembered Maria Lorenza as she had once been. The two of them as children, climbing trees, chasing through the barley fields, laughing. Her whispered jests and giggles in their father's chapel, when they were meant to be solemn. Her tears, the raw fear in her eyes, when Matteo Strozzi had betrayed her and she had only Orlando to turn to.

Maria Lorenza had been there as long as Orlando could remember. His sweet, beautiful baby sister. She never deserved the torment that had driven her to this.

A baby's piercing cry suddenly broke the silence of the church. Orlando pushed himself to his feet and turned to see one of the nuns standing in the doorway. Maria's new daughter was cradled in her arms, a fragile new life that bloomed in the face of her mother's death. His niece, who had only him now to look after her. Who had lost her mother in the most horrible of ways. Maria had been so sure she could not look after her child, that the shame of having a bastard daughter would drown them both, and thus she had chosen to leave them all. She could bear the humiliation no longer.

Matteo Strozzi had caused all of this. And he would pay. Orlando would make sure of that.

Chapter One

The Tuscan countryside—spring 1478

My Most Illustrious Lords:
My brother Giuliano has just been killed and my government is in the greatest danger. Now is the time, my lords, to help your servant Lorenzo. Send all the troops you can with all speed, so that they may be the shield and safety of my state, just as they have always been.

Your servitor, Lorenzo de' Medici.

Letter to the Lords of Milan, April 26, 1478

'In a short time passes every great rain; and the warmth makes disappear the snows and ice that make the rivers look so proud; nor was the sky ever covered by so thick a cloud that, meeting the fury of the winds, it did not flee from the hills and the valleys.'

The girl's voice, reading from the volume of Petrarch, flowed low and sweet on the warm breeze. It mingled with the hum of bees, seeking the most luscious of the early summer flowers, with the twitter and chatter of birds. The wind whistled through the gnarled branches of the heavy-laden olive trees and the tall cypresses. It was the slowest, most lazy of days. Steps grew heavy in the sunlight, laughter rich. Work was only an afterthought.

Perfect for Isabella's own task. There were few tasks for her to undertake at her father's villa. Meals were lighter, the rich curtains and carpets of winter folded away and replaced by thin, airy linens. The servants gossiped by the open windows, peeling vegetables for a light pottage as the chickens, their feathery lives spared for the moment, scratched in the dirt of the back courtyard. No, she would not be expected at home until sundown, when her father stirred from his books and began wondering where his supper was.

Isabella leaned over her sketchbook, easing the side of her thumb to smudge a harsh charcoal line. 'The fury of the winds...' The girl's voice faltered.

Isabella glanced up to find that Veronica, their neighbour's young daughter, still sat in her spot of sun, the book she was reading from open on her lap. She was a perfect model, with her pale golden curls limned by the sun into a halo, her oval face lightly touched with the bronze of summer. Her pink-striped skirts spread around her on the grass like the ruffled petals of a rose against leaves. But, by St Catherine, the girl would not sit still!

'What is it, Veronica?' she asked.

'May I see the drawing yet, *madonna*?' the child said, eagerness hidden low in her gentle voice. 'We have been sitting here for ever so long!'

Long? Isabella glanced at the azure sky above

them to see that the slant of the light had changed subtly, its rays shifting to a deep caramel. The *sfumato* of morning, that silvery-grey haze so peculiar to hot Tuscan days, had long ago burned off. Yet to Isabella, so absorbed in capturing the girl's face on parchment, infusing the cold, black lines with Veronica's sweet, innocent spirit, it seemed only moments had passed.

'All the better to practise your reading, Veronica,' she said, placing her charcoal back in its specially slotted box and flexing her fingers. Her skin and nails were stained deep grey, so engrained that surely she could not scrub it clean before her father saw. Ah, well. After all these years of living alone together, he was accustomed to her doings, as she was to his.

'You read that poem so beautifully,' she continued. 'Your parents will be very proud.'

Veronica closed the precious, green leather-bound book and held it tightly to her stomach, a shy smile touching her rosebud lips. 'Do you think so, *madonna*? They say I must go to my aunt's house in Florence once the summer is over, to learn to be a true lady and find a suitable betrothal.' She glanced uncertainly down at the book. 'I shouldn't like to shame myself there.'

Ah, Florence. Isabella repressed a flash of envy, of longing. Surely it was foolish to be jealous of a child, when she herself was a great, grown lady of nineteen! But to see the treasures of Florence, the art of Bellini, Botticelli, Ghirlandaio, the glorious churches and galleries and *palazzi*—it must be great indeed. A glory of unsurpassed beauty, of vast sophistication. A world completely unlike their quiet country existence.

It was a world she knew only from her cousin Caterina's letters and likely to remain that way for as long as her widowed father needed her. After he had lost her mother so many years before, he'd retreated into his own world of books and was likely to stay there, grieving over his wife. Isabella never wanted to face that herself.

'Then we shall gift them with this drawing

before you leave,' Isabella told Veronica. 'But you cannot see it just yet! Not until it is finished.'

Veronica sighed deeply with disappointment and Isabella laughed at her pout. Surely the child had a long distance to go before she found that betrothal and set to running her own household! Much like Isabella, who was long past the age to marry, but who couldn't imagine being a wife. She liked being herself far too much to submit to the will of a husband.

And she had watched what had happened to her father when her beautiful mother died all those years ago. The way he had retreated into himself, giving into the grief of losing his wife so completely he even forgot he had a daughter for a time. She could not bear to feel thus herself. Her art took all her emotion.

'Run along now, little bird,' Isabella said. 'Your mama will be looking for you.'

Veronica stood up, shaking out her skirts, the book tucked beneath her arm. 'Shall we meet again tomorrow, *madonna*?'

'Of course, if it does not rain. We want to finish this before you go, no?'

Veronica gave her one last giggle, then spun around and dashed out of the sunny grove, her gown a pink blur until she disappeared down a slope towards her parents' villa.

Isabella slid a thin piece of paper over the sketch to keep it from smudging before carefully closing the book. The pages were almost full now, the pristine whiteness covered with black-and-grey images of flowers, trees, houses, people, imaginary scenes. Anything that caught her eye and challenged her to capture its essence in lines and planes.

She packed the precious volume carefully in a basket, along with her charcoal box and the remains of a long-consumed picnic meal. She would have to leave soon, as well, and abandon this secret, enchanted grove for the prosaic real world of the villa. Her father would be emerging from his library, looking about for her in his absent way.

Not just yet, though. Isabella lay back in the

warm grass, staring up at the sky through the long, lacy pattern of the olive branches. The bright blue of afternoon had faded to a paler, rose-tinged hue, but the air still hung heavy, not yet cooled by the onrush of evening. She smelled the green freshness of the grass, the sulphur-tinged sweetness of wild jasmine. It was a beautiful time of day, her favourite, when it seemed she was all alone in the world, that nothing could touch her, hurt her, change her. There were no responsibilities, no demands. No wild longings.

Isabella closed her eyes, feeling the soft caress of the wind across her cheeks, through the fall of her loose, thick black hair. The song of the birds was muted now, as if they were far away. What would it be like to fly free as they did, to feel the breeze bearing her up, up, up? To soar above the earth.

She imagined a painting in her mind, a canvas washed with an expanse of clear, priceless sky-blue, dotted with grey-tipped white clouds. At the very bottom of the scene, a string of buildings, villas, farms, the dome of a church. Perhaps the tiny dots of people going about their daily business. And above, hovering in the heady, thin air of perfect freedom, Icarus. A handsome young man, naked but for the pointed wings arcing above his head. A single moment of untainted glory. But high above, at the top edge of the canvas, the hot, waiting rays of the harsh sun. The fall that lurked for all men who dared fly too high.

Isabella opened her eyes and for an instant she fancied she saw a tiny figure soaring towards the sunset. His face was indistinct, she couldn't yet envision it, though she dreamed of just such a man. Somewhere out there, waiting for her.

She laughed wryly. That was hardly likely. Their home here was beautiful, safe, tucked far away from the dangerous doings of the great men in Florence. The men of her Strozzi cousins' circle. There were no dangerous suns here. But neither were there wax wings to bear a soul to freedom.

The sky was streaked with vivid orange and gold now, a paint palette that signalled the close of one more day. She had stayed here too long.

Isabella pushed herself up, rising slowly to her feet. Her legs were stiff from sitting too long, from balancing the sketchbook on her knees. Her dark blue skirts were streaked with ochre-coloured dust and grass blades, but she had no time to worry about that now. She had to get home, to make sure supper was waiting for her father.

The farm was slowly coming to life for the evening, after the long siesta of the sleepy afternoon. Outside the cottages, tables were being set up beneath the trees, candles lit against the gathering darkness. Children raced around, energized by the cool breeze that crept over the dusty land, banishing the heat of the day. Laughter, the barking of dogs, the fresh song of awakening night birds followed Isabella as she hurried down the pathway, dirt billowing around her sandal-clad feet, the hem of her gown.

'Buona notte!' people called after her and she answered with quick waves, smiles. At last she came to the top of the slope that led to her father's villa.

It was quieter there, the ebb and flow of life in the rough stone cottages muffled by a ring of scrubby olive trees, and by something else, something intangible yet ever-present. The barrier of being different. Her father's family had lived on this estate for decades, had overseen the fields, the orchards, the grapevines. Isabella had known all those people since she was in swaddling clothes, the poor little *bambina* with no mother who thus became the child of all. Or none.

But truly they *were* different. She and her father. The scholar, the man so wrapped in his dusty books, his ancient world, his memories of her mother, that he never walked the fields as his own father had. He cared little for the things that absorbed the days of others, the mundane work of feeding families, worshipping God, living life. And she, his daughter, his only child, was worse. A woman who would rather scribble strange images on parchment than marry and raise children.

Isabella absently twisted her untidy black hair up into a knot, thinking of the whispers people thought she couldn't hear. This was her home, the only one she had ever known. Yet she didn't belong here. She thought again of Icarus, soaring free on his fatal wings. What she would not give for just a taste of that freedom! Yet it was impossible. She was a woman, she had her duties, her destinies. Wings could not be hers.

But there was one choice she *could* make, a gift of her father's hazy unworldliness, his carelessness. She could choose not to marry some country lordling and lose her youth and vitality in endless tasks, endless childbearing. Even if it meant she stayed frozen for ever.

Isabella secured her hair with a comb from her pocket, brushed off her skirts and tugged the ruffled cuffs of her chemise down to cover the worst of the charcoal smudges. She was as tidy as she could make herself, so she continued on her way down the shadowed slope towards the villa.

Their house had once been the grandest in the neighbourhood, back in her grandfather's youth, when it was newly built. The latest design, with all the most modern conveniences, the most luxurious furnishings. Her grandmother was a great beauty, a daughter of the Strozzi family, and she gave banquets and dances that were talked of even in Florence.

That was a long time ago.

Isabella's grandparents had been gone for many years and under her father's stewardship the villa had fallen silent. Isabella heard tell that her mother, another Strozzi, had also given banquets, had danced under the moonlight with all her stylish Florentine friends. But she'd died at Isabella's birth and that sparkling life ended for all of them. Her father detested dancing without his wife, was indifferent to food and feasting. Oh, they did sometimes have guests to be sure, other scholars who came to debate with her father over the philosophies of the ancient

Greeks, the concepts of higher mathematics, the nature of man's highest vocation.

They did not care for dancing, either. Or even for the art that was Isabella's life-sustaining joy. And her mother's relatives had no use for a connection who was only a scholar, no use in a battle or at forming new alliances.

The house came into view at last and Isabella paused to catch her breath at the edge of the wild, overgrown garden. When the villa was new-built, it had been a deep ochre colour, thickly stuccoed, set off by the green-painted shutters and carved wooden doors. Now it was faded to the uneven colour of a ripe peach, the stucco flaking away in places to reveal the stone beneath, the shutters peeling. A few of the terracotta tiles of the roof were missing and the garden where Isabella's mother had danced was a wild snarl. Statuary that once came all the way from Rome tilted this way and that amid the tangled vines, the haphazard spill of flowers. A chipped Cupid with bow drawn, a smiling Venus, Neptune with no trident.

The windows of the upper floors were dark, blank, but the doors were open, casting golden light out into the courtyard. The lower windows were thrown wide to the twilight breeze and Isabella could hear the laughter and chatter of the servants as they finished preparing supper. A table was set up near the old fountain, laid out with pitchers of wine, loaves of fresh-baked breads and ewers of olive oil.

The conversation was a high hum, an ebb and flow, but it became clearer as Isabella moved ever closer to the open doors, coalescing into words.

'...wasn't sure his grand relations even remembered he was here,' she heard the cook, Flavia, say. The woman's comments were punctuated with the click of pottery bowls. 'He hasn't heard from them in months.'

'And a messenger came today?' Mena, the housekeeper who also served as Isabella's maid, said.

A messenger? Isabella paused, her foot on the stone step. Flavia was right—they seldom heard from their relations, not that there were many of them left. Her father's family was not a fertile one and her mother's cousins, the Strozzis, were people of high position in Florence. Isabella had only met them a few times, and knew little about them except that their lives sounded like a dream of beauty and culture. Why would they send a messenger now?

'I saw him myself,' one of the footmen commented. 'Very grand, in a livery of blue-and-cream velvet.'

'The Strozzi colours,' Mena murmured. 'What would they want now? I did hear…'

Her words were shattered by the crash of a falling bowl, the excited bark of one of the kitchen dogs.

'Maledizione!' Flavia cursed.

Isabella glanced back over her shoulder, as if she could see the 'grand' messenger, but there was only the empty garden.

'Signorina Isabella!' Mena called, startling Isabella back to the present moment, the reality of her place. Her head whipped back around to find Mena standing before her in the doorway, balancing a large bowl of boiled greens. 'So, here you are at last. Are you quite all right?'

Isabella blinked at her, the woman's familiar, creased, olive-complexioned face coming into focus. Her dark eyes were narrow with concern. Isabella gave her a reassuring smile. 'I am very well, Mena. Just a bit too much sun, I think.'

Mena gave a disapproving cluck and moved around Isabella to set the bowl on the waiting table. 'You spend far too much time wandering about outdoors, *signorina*. Soon you will be dark as a Moor!'

Isabella laughed. 'I hardly think it matters! No one will see me, dark or fair. Besides, I need the light for my work.'

Mena tossed her a speculative glance but said nothing. She merely made that clucking sound again, a symbol of disapproval Isabella had known since she was a babe in arms. 'Go fetch the pottage.'

Isabella nodded and stepped into the kitchen. The heat of the cooking fires hit her in the face, thick and humid after the cooling evening air, filled with the scents of roasted chicken, spices, boiling vegetables, burned sugar.

Flavia, a plump, red-faced woman who had also been with their family for as long as Isabella could remember, was stirring a vat of stewed chicken in cinnamon. She merely nodded towards the pottage and Isabella snatched it up to carry it back outside, away from the scalding heat.

Mena lingered by the table, pouring wine into pottery goblets. As Isabella set down the pottage, she leaned close and whispered, 'Cousin Caterina sent a letter?'

Mena did not meet her gaze. She shrugged, fussing with the wine. 'A letter *did* come, but who can name the sender?'

'Mena! How many other Strozzis do we know? What do you think she wants?'

Mena's lips tightened. She was a country woman, bred of sturdy Tuscan stock, and had lived all her life in this spot. She knew little of Florentine doings, and what she did know she disapproved of. Learning old, pagan ways, looking at paintings of naked goddesses and gods—it went against God and the saints. Even as she loved Isabella, had practically raised her after her mother died, Isabella knew well she did not understand Isabella's longing for a life that was not her own.

'Oh, *signorina*,' Mena said, strangely sad. 'Why can you not just…?'

'Is this my supper?' a puzzled voice enquired, thin, confused.

Isabella gave Mena one more searching look, but it was obvious that the maid knew no more of their mysterious messenger. She had only lectures about appreciating one's place in the world, the place where God placed one. Isabella had heard it all before.

She glanced over to see her father standing at the edge of the garden. It was his practice every evening to emerge from his library when it grew too dark to see the pages of his books and wander out the front doors around the house until he found someone to tell him what to do, where to go. It was no use to have servants remind him of the time, or guide him to the supper table—the same table they ate at every night.

Isabella smiled at him gently. His long, white hair stood out in a thick, uneven corona around his round, ruddy face and his beard was too long, his brows wild above faded green-grey eyes. The green-grey eyes Isabella inherited. Despite the warmth of summer, he wore an old, patched velvet robe trimmed with moth-eaten fur.

'*Sì*, Father, it is your supper,' she said, hurrying over to slip her arm through his and lead him to his chair.

'Vegetables?' he asked, absently surveying the offerings.

'And some stewed chicken with cinnamon,' said Isabella, sitting down next to him. 'You like cinnamon. Flavia is just finishing with it.'

'I will go fetch it,' Mena said and left them to return to the kitchen. The hum of voices resumed in there as Isabella pressed a cup of wine into her father's hand. How she yearned to ask him about the letter, to discover what was happening with their Florence relations! But she knew full well it would never work to press him. Until her father had some food, some wine, emerged from his dream world of study, he would not even remember what she talked about.

'How was your day?' she asked, spooning out a portion of the pottage on to his plate. 'Did you finish the new essay on the *Aeneid*?'

'No, no, not yet. But I am close, I think. Very close. I must write to Fernando in Mantua. He has documents that will be of great use to me in this matter.'

'Perhaps he would even travel here himself, then you could discuss it in person,' Isabella said. 'We have not seen him in many months.'

'Hmm,' was all her father said.

Mena returned with the chicken and they ate in silence as the night shadows lengthened and the stars emerged above them. It was a clear, cool evening, the moon a mere silvery sliver on the horizon. Gradually, Isabella felt the tension of the day easing from her shoulders, sliding away on wine and serene silence. When the dessert of rice cooked in honey and almond milk was consumed, the lanterns strung high in the trees were lit and Isabella and her father were left alone. The conversation in the kitchen slowed, until there was only the distant song of the nightingale.

Isabella leaned her chin in her hand and closed her eyes, envisioning the sketch of young Veronica. There was still something not quite right about the line of the cheek, the flow of the hair, something she could not quite decipher…

'Perhaps I *shall* invite Fernando to visit,' her father suddenly said.

Isabella's eyes flew open. 'What? Father, I mentioned that above an hour ago!'

Her father just smiled. 'Ah, Bella, you think I do not listen to you. I do. It simply takes time for me to absorb your words.'

Isabella laughed and reached out to pour more wine into their goblets. 'That is very good to know, Father. And, yes, it will be a fine thing to have your friend here for a visit. He could help you so much with your studies. I fear you must find it a lonely task, with none to share your interests.'

'I enjoy the quiet,' he answered and took a slow sip of his wine. 'After the great clamour at university so long ago, I found that only peace is conducive to true study. Do you not find it so, Bella, in your own work?'

Isabella frowned, puzzled. She did not know her father even realized she *had* 'work'. 'My art?'

'Hmm, yes. Oh, but then art is different from history. I deal with men who are dead, events that are dust. Art is—well, it is life. How can you progress here, when there is nothing to inspire you? No one to help you?'

Isabella was utterly astonished. Every evening, winter or summer, rain or star-shine, she and her father supped together here at this table. Yet these were the greatest number of words they had shared in a long while, the most true understanding he had ever shown her. He loved her, she knew that. He just lived so much in his own mind. 'I am content,' she said.

'Content. But not happy.' Her father slowly shook his head, his wild hair drooping over his wrinkled brow. 'Bella, I forget how young you are. This is the life I want, the life I have chosen. You deserve the chance to choose, as well. To look beyond our home and perhaps find a new way. A fine husband. A wider world.' He sighed. 'You are really so much like your mother.'

'Father, what has brought this on?' Isabella asked, bewildered. 'Are we *not* content here together? Are you…?' A horrible thought struck her. 'Are you ill?'

He laughed. 'Not at all. Just the aches and pains of age. I merely had a reminder of the outside world today. A reminder long overdue.' He reached inside his robe and withdrew a small scroll. The blue wax seal was broken.

Ah, yes. The letter from Caterina, the letter

that caused such a furore of curiosity in their house. 'What is that, Father?'

'A letter from your cousin Caterina Strozzi. She writes to enquire after you.' He unrolled the scroll, flattening it on the table. 'She has shown an interest in you before, but, well, with relations such as they were between myself and her father, how useless I was to them after your mother died—I thought it better to leave things alone.'

'What has changed?' Isabella asked.

'Caterina writes that she knows of your great interest in art, an interest that the two of you share. She says she has not been well of late and she would like a companion to help her, to be her friend. Someone she could trust, a kinswoman. She asks if you will come to live with her in Florence. For a time, anyway.'

Live in Florence? Isabella's stomach seized and fluttered with a sudden, icy rush of joy and fear. She turned away, pressing her hands hard to that ache. Could this be real? It was what she longed for, prayed for! A wider world, a journey to a place of art and beauty and culture, where she would no longer be alone. Her greatest wish, held out to her now, a gleaming jewel she had only to reach out for.

And yet—and yet…

This was her home, all she knew. What if her bright dream tarnished, turned to ashes in the harsh glare of real life? And what if the nightmares she'd had when she was younger came to torment her in the new house? They hadn't visited her in a long time, but when she was tired or worried, the visions came back. What would she do then?

'It is entirely up to you, Bella,' her father said quietly. 'Florence was poison for me, but it could be good for you. You are so smart, so lovely. But if you do not wish to go, that is very well, too.'

'Who would take care of you, Father?' she whispered, still surrounded by that buzzing brilliance of unreality.

'Why, the servants, of course! You could take Mena with you, but the rest of us will rub along well enough. My needs are few. And I will invite some of those friends to visit. It is past time I did that anyway.' He reached out suddenly and took her hand, his fingers gnarled, ink-stained, gentle. 'I cannot stand in your way any longer, Bella. You must find your own path now.'

Isabella curled her hand around his tightly. 'Is my path in Florence?'

He nodded. 'I think it may be.'

She drew in a deep, steadying breath. All her trepidation, her wild fears, unspooled like a skein of wool and floated free. This was right. This was her destiny, what she waited for all her nineteen years. She laughed aloud, her heart alight with all the shimmering possibilities of the future.

'Very well, then!' she cried. 'I will go to Florence.'

'There is the sea and who will drain it dry? Precious as silver, inexhaustible, ever-new, it breeds the more we reap it—tides on tides of crimson dye our robes blood-red...'

Orlando Landucci stared out of the window into the Florence dusk, barely hearing the soft voice of Lucretia, his former mistress and now his friend, as she read from the *Oresteia*. Evening was gathering fast, always the most beautiful time in the city. A moment when the stone towers turned to spun gold in the torchlight, when ordinary faces turned mysterious and beautiful. All the filth and ugliness were hidden away in the darkness. And so were wicked deeds.

He could hide, too, could forget, even if it was only for few hours. He loved the night.

But tonight the veil was very thin and he couldn't lose himself in the illicit pleasures of Florence as he usually did. Trouble was bubbling just below Florence's serene, elegant surface. A tension that simmered and crackled, soon to snap and release the winged evils of Pandora's box into the world. None of them could deceive themselves much longer. Not even the great Medici and their allies.

Soon Orlando would also have his chance. He wouldn't have to hide in the night any longer.

As the twilight slipped into black darkness, the fine cobblestone square below Lucretia's window transformed. Respectable families retreated behind the stout walls of their *palazzi*, closing their shutters. Merchants shut their shops in the *mercato* and beggars took refuge in church doorways.

Yet Florence was far from forsaken. Soon the *calles* would fill with new crowds, young men in brightly striped hose and pearl-sewn doublets, plumed velvet caps on their curled hair. They sang bawdy songs as they passed wine flasks between them, waiting for the courtesans in their crimson-and-yellow satins to emerge from their houses. Music could be heard in the distance, flutes and tambours, a merry dance that grew louder and louder as the night became darker.

Suddenly, as he watched lazily, a large group tumbled into the square, led by the musicians. At their head was the greatest rogue in all

Florence, Giuliano de Medici, the handsome younger brother of the all-powerful Lorenzo, followed by his ever-present friends.

They had obviously started on the strong wine a long time before, for they stumbled on the paving stones, laughing uproariously as one of them tumbled to his knees. Their voices, raised in out-of-tune song, floated up to Orlando's window. They spun and flowed in a stained-glass kaleidoscope of bright greens, blues, reds, waving plumes and flashing jewels. Like a painting come to life.

Orlando eased the window open an inch, letting in the music and laughter, borne on a cool, perfume-scented breeze that seemed to spread their merriment to every corner of the city. There was no danger yet to their merriment, no sadness, no dread. Only their youthful, privileged certainty that all would be well for them, that beauty and merriment would always prevail.

Orlando had once been just like them. So sure nothing could touch the brightness of his life.

Now he knew how very false that was. How delicate, like a puff of dust blown away by a hot summer wind. They soon would know that, too.

He saw Eleanora Melozzi hung on Giuliano's velvet-clad arm, the most expensive courtesan in all Florence. The torchlight glowed on the loose fall of her golden hair as she turned to laugh with the couple who tripped behind them.

The red-haired woman who was Eleanora's friend held on to a tall, fair-haired man's arm, her jewelled hand curled tight and possessive around his velvet sleeve. He threw back his head in a burst of raucous laughter, a ray of flickering light falling over his face.

It was Matteo Strozzi.

Orlando's fist tightened on the edge of the window until the glass bit into his skin. He felt it not at all. He could only see Strozzi, the vile bastard. The man he had vowed to destroy.

Suddenly, through his crimson haze of anger, he felt a soft touch on his sleeve, drawing his hand down. Startled out of his anger, he looked down to see that Lucretia had left her book and come to his side. She stared up at him, her green-gold eyes wide with concern.

He flashed a quick grin, trying to reassure her. He didn't want anyone to know the secret fury that burned inside of him. Lucretia had been his first mistress when he was a wild youth and now that she was retired she was his friend. Her *palazzo* was a place where he could go for gentle quiet and for someone to talk to, share his love of books and art. Lucretia knew him too well to be put off by a careless smile, a teasing word, as everyone else was. Florence was city of facades and Orlando was a master of them.

'You are very distracted this evening, Orlando *caro*,' she said. 'What is amiss?'

He knew he couldn't fool Lucretia, but neither could he confide in her tonight. The wild darkness was wrapping around him, seizing hold of him, and soon he would be lost to it. Only rougher pleasures could drown it tonight.

He laughed and wrapped his arm around Lucretia's waist, drawing her closer until her jasmine scent drowned out the night breeze. 'What could be amiss on a night such as this, my fair Lucretia? The stars are like diamonds, sprinkled in your beautiful hair…'

'You are a terrible poet.' Lucretia laughed, but her gaze slid to the street below, where the merry Medici retinue was retreating from the square. 'Were you thinking of them?'

'Why would I do that? Everyone else thinks of them. At least one thought in this city must be for something else.'

Lucretia frowned. 'My friend Jacopo Pazzi says…'

'Something he has no business saying in front of you, I am sure,' Orlando said. He didn't want to think of Matteo Strozzi or his friends the Medicis, not now. The old wildness was coming over him again. He, too, knew some of the Pazzi family, the great, wealthy rivals of the Medici, and he knew how indiscreet they could be when the wine flowed. It was very dangerous. 'Men's discontent grows when they are in their cups, as you know better than anyone, my Lucretia.'

She still stared down at the square, where the Medici—and Matteo Strozzi—had been. They seemed to leave a shadow behind them. But she said nothing more about them. 'I do wish you would come with me to Bianca's tonight. She has a new pet poet, they say he is very amusing. It could distract you.'

'I fear not, *bella* Lucretia. I've already agreed to another engagement with some friends.'

Lucretia laughed. 'An engagement at a disreputable tavern outside the city walls? Are we too refined for you now, Orlando?'

A tavern was exactly where he was going, but he wouldn't admit that to Lucretia, who had once been the most educated, most witty courtesan in all the city. He loved the cultured life she created around herself and her friends. But some nights, when the dark demons were creeping up on him, grabbing at him with their cold, skeletal fingers, only rougher pleasures could distract him. Cheap wine, pretty women, rude music.

'Oh, Orlando,' she said with a laugh. 'One day you will find whatever it is you seek and it will make you want to be a better man. You are like a questing knight.'

'Me?' he scoffed, laughing. 'A questing knight? I search for a fresh barrel of ale, mayhap, but a rare jewel? You have become a romantic in your retirement, I fear.'

She shook her head. 'I know you. One day you will see, I promise you that. And your life will change.'

'I will see you next week, Lucretia,' he said. He took her bejewelled hand and raised it to his lips.

She gently touched his cheek. A sad little smile touched her lips. 'I do hope so. I worry about you, Orlando, when you get that look in your eyes.'

'No need to worry about me, *bella*,' he said, trying to give a careless laugh.

But it was obvious Lucretia was not fooled.

She stepped back and waved him away. 'Go, then, if you must! You young men and your taverns…'

Orlando kissed her once more, and strode out of her elegant *palazzo* and into the increasingly crowded streets. He slipped on a black half-mask and made sure his daggers were strapped at his belt. The crowds grew thicker, louder, the farther he went into the city's centre. The houses were taller, packed closer together until the stucco walls nearly touched above his head. The window shutters were thrown open to the night, women in loose *camicie* and bright gowns leaning out to call down to passers-by. The smell of cheap ale and rose water hung in the warm air. Only in a place such as this could Orlando forget what had happened to Maria Lorenza. Only there could he be free.

Yet that freedom never lasted long. The demons always caught up with him in the end.

Chapter Two

'*Pesce, pesce*! The finest, freshest fish in all of Florence, *madonna*, you will not be sorry.'

Isabella laughed at the fishmonger's solicitations, waving him away as she guided her horse around the edges of the *mercato*. He shrugged and turned to the next passer-by and soon the acrid scent of fish rotting in the sun faded behind her, giving way to the sweetness of ripe fruit, the spiciness of cinnamon-coated nuts.

How odd, she mused, *to find something so prosaic as fish in such a dreamland.*

Ever since they'd entered through one of Florence's twelve gates, the Gate of Fortune, and headed towards the Strozzi *palazzo*, Isabella felt caught up in a swirling fantasy, a land she could not have summoned up even on a canvas. Descriptions in books, and from her father's friends, could never fully conjure such a place.

It was slow going on their horses; Isabella was trailed by Mena and two footmen, plus mules for their baggage. It gave her time to stare, to inhale deeply of the scents and sights, to absorb all of it into herself. She had to remember all of this, all the faces and facades, so she could commit it to her sketchbook. Then one day, when she was an old woman buried again in the country, she could gaze at the faded drawings and remember the day she came fully to life.

Florence was a city of twisting streets, some of them so narrow she and her party were forced to move in single file, their horses' hooves clacking on the uneven flagstones. There were open squares, tall towers, fortresslike *palazzi* with massive, unbreachable stone walls, over-hanging balconies where beautifully dressed ladies lounged and laughed on this sunny day, their hair spread out to catch the golden rays.

The old churches, silent and dignified in their

ancient sanctity, presented facades of geometrical patterns of faded marble in black, white, green, pink. Behind them were high, crowded buildings where the workers and artisans lived, bursting with shouts, cries, shrieks of laughter. Behind *them* were convents and abbeys, barred, secure, mysterious.

The sheer *life* of the place was overwhelming. Isabella was used to her Tuscan home, a place where olive trees outnumbered people, where quiet contemplation reigned. Here, a rich cacophony blended and echoed all around. The patter of merchants selling fabric, vegetables, candles, feathers, perfumes. The pleas of beggars, the screams of children chasing down the *calles*, the barking of stray dogs, and snorts of pigs as they were led to market. It was crowded, hot, the air close with the smells of cooking meat, spilled wine, pungent perfumes, unwashed skin, sweet flowers in hidden courtyards.

Isabella loved it. She adored every reeking, noisy fragment of it all. Her heart lifted in her breast, rising up on those first tentative wings of freedom she had thought never to find. Life had been waiting here all along, in these narrow streets of Florence.

Isabella twisted her head around to study a church tower laid out in an intricate pattern of coloured marbles, all green and pink and bright white in the sun. She wished she had her sketchbook with her, so she could capture the lines and shapes of it all. It held her spellbound for a long moment.

She heard a shout somewhere ahead of her and spun back around, startled. Mena and the others had vanished and all around her was the press of strangers. People jostling together, roughly dressed, loudly laughing.

She felt a sudden cold stab of panic. At home she wandered alone everywhere, but those were fields and vineyards, her own gardens. This place that had seemed so beautiful and enticing only a moment ago suddenly seemed frightening, strange, an alien world, and she had no idea how to make her way in it.

She steered her horse down a narrower, quieter street. She tried to remember Caterina's letter, which was tucked up now in one of the footmen's saddlebags, the location of her cousins' *palazzo*, but suddenly all the lovely buildings that held her so captivated seemed so very alike. The children who dashed past, the women who peered out from behind latticed windows, seemed as if they watched her with suspicions.

Confused and growing a little frightened, Isabella turned another corner and found herself in a small courtyard, tall houses leanings in on all sides, casting a shadow on the cracked cobblestones under her horse's hooves. These buildings were certainly not as fine as the ones that lined the river. The plasterwork was flaking, the windows free of fine glass and velvet curtains, and the fountain at its centre was broken and silent. Surely this was far from where Caterina lived.

She tugged on the reins to turn the horse. But the entrance to the courtyard was blocked by two men she hadn't noticed before and it angered her that she had let her guard down. They were both tall, brawny in their rough russet doublets, their bearded faces shadowed. One of them grinned at her, a horrible flash of yellowed, broken teeth behind his black beard.

'Look what pretty little bird just landed here,' the smiler said. His companion just grunted, which seemed even more fearsome.

'*Scusi, signor,*' Isabella murmured, keeping her head high even though she was shivering. She tightened her grip on the reins and tried to slide past them in the narrow passageway.

It all happened in an instant. One of the men reached up and grabbed her horse's bridle and the other seized her arm in a bruising grip. He dragged her towards him and a sharp bolt of pain shot all down her side. She screamed and tried to kick out at him, but her skirts wrapped around her legs. She managed to catch his cheek with her nails and he cursed and drew back his fist.

Just as suddenly as she was attacked, the man who held on to her was wrenched away and she stumbled over the uneven cobblestones. Her hat tumbled from its anchoring pins and blinded her for a moment. She felt dizzy, nauseated, as the sound of shouts and a loud, bruising thud hit her ears.

Isabella tossed her hat aside and shook back the tangle of her loosened hair. The scene that flashed in front of her was like something in a painting, a judgement fresco in a church, a violent swirl of movement and blurred faces against a swirl of colour. She instinctively scrambled out of the way and pressed herself tight to a stucco wall as she tried to make sense of what was happening right before her horrified eyes.

One of her would-be attackers lay still on the cobbles, a dark stain spreading beneath him. The other man was locked in combat with a tall figure all in black, like some avenging spirit. He moved with a terrible grace, as if mortal combat was nothing to him at all, his fists and booted feet like lethal weapons that looked so elegant and moved with sudden, sharp force.

The man who had tried to attack her landed with a horribly soft crack on the stones near his cohort. He scrambled to his feet with an inhuman cry, lifted up his groaning companion under the shoulders and the two of them fled from the deserted courtyard. In their wake there was an almost deafening silence, where the sound of the dark angel's breath seemed to rush past her like feathered wings.

Isabella was astonished, appalled—and fascinated. How had the world changed around her so suddenly?

She wanted to flee, to run and hide from the sudden violence and fear that had grabbed hold of her and shaken her. Yet somehow she was held there, staring at him in astonishment.

Her rescuer slowly turned to look directly at her and she bit her lip to hold back a gasp. He did look like an angel in truth, a fallen angel. Glossy dark hair was tumbled over his forehead and a bleeding cut arced across his sun-bronzed cheek, but nothing could detract from that strangely otherworldly beauty. His face was all austere, sharply carved angles, his lips full and sensual, just as she would paint an angel in need of redemption.

But his eyes—his eyes were a bright, pale sea-green, almost glowing in the shadowed courtyard. She glimpsed a flash of something in them that spoke to her of his deep-down soul, something dark and haunted. She knew she should be afraid, but somehow she was not at all. She wanted to move nearer to him, to touch that hair and look into those eyes. She pressed herself back harder to the cold wall, as it seemed to be the only thing holding her up in that moment.

He swiped his narrow black sleeve over his damp brow. It was the only sign it had taken him any effort at all to dispatch two brigands. 'Are you hurt, *signorina*?' he asked. His voice was rough, deep, but calm.

She swallowed hard past the dry knot in her throat. 'I—nay. You came upon us very quickly. I can't thank you enough. I—I was lost, you see, and those men…'

A faint, reassuring smile touched his lips. 'You should be very careful where you go in Florence, *signorina*. These streets can be most deceptive.'

Isabella thought of the sparkling beauty of the river, the bright life that had surrounded her there. How swiftly it all ended. And now—now there was this man in front of her. A man such as she had never seen before.

'I see that now,' she said simply. All the words she had ever known seemed to have fled. Was this how it was for her parents when they met, struck dumb by each other? She had to be very careful.

He took a step towards her and held out his hand. He appeared to be trying to move very slowly, very carefully, as if she was a wild animal he had to calm. 'Come, let me see you home. I assure you, I mean you no harm as these men did.'

Somehow, she believed him, even against all that she had just seen. He had been so violent with those men, but now—now there was only that pale light in those extraordinary eyes. She gave a rueful laugh. 'I am not sure where that is. I have only just arrived in the city.'

Disbelief flashed across his sculpted face. 'But you must have family here.'

'I do, but…' Her words trailed away as she was beset by new doubts. She wasn't sure she should mention her cousins, tell him where she was going.

He gave a short nod, as if he understood. 'Come, I will find a guard to see you where you wish to go. Someone we can both trust.'

That did not sound a great deal safer. After all, his guards would surely know where she went. But she could see no other alternative. She had to find Caterina somehow and she certainly did not want to wander into another brawl. She studied his face carefully for a moment. That flash of darkness she had glimpsed in him was gone now, covered in a small smile, but she remembered it had been there and it made her shiver.

'Thank you,' she said. 'I am in your debt, *signor.*'

He shook his head. 'I have now done my good deed for the day.'

'And need no more penance now?' she asked, surprising herself.

He looked surprised for an instant. 'I must always do penance, *signorina*. But come now, we will find someone to see you safely home…'

'Signorina Isabella! Thank the saints you are safe,' Isabella heard Mena cry from the thick crowd around the cathedral of Santa Maria del Fiore, where her dark angel's two guards had led her safely. They looked much as her original attackers had, brawny, bearded men, but they were silent and courteous, watchful of everything that went on as they took her from the tavern where her rescuer had found them. She had no idea who they were, but they had listened to the man closely, nodded and taken her here, to the most crowded place in the city. She did not even know their names.

Nor did she know her angel's name, or anything about him but the fascination she had
glimpsed in his face so briefly. She would not
forget him, she was sure. That was a face she
would see in her dreams.

But would she ever see it again in real life?
She longed to—and yet she feared to at the
same time.

'Mena!' she cried, straining up in the stir-
rups until she could see her maid pushing the
crowd aside to make her way towards Isabella.
A vast relief flooded over her, warm and familiar. 'There you are!'

'You vanished and we could not find you!' the
maid said, tears on her wrinkled cheeks. 'This
place is wicked. We should go home.'

'We cannot go without seeing Caterina,' Isabella said. She thought it better not to tell Mena
all that had happened. There had been too much
darkness in the day already. She only wanted
to find her cousins' home, have a bath and a
meal—and think about her rescuer. Sketch his

face before she could forget it. 'These men helped me find my way...'

She glanced back, but her guards had gone, melted away as if they had never been her silent escort at all. Had she only dreamed the whole strange scene? It had happened before.

But, no. She remembered all too well the touch of her rescuer's hand on her skin, the glow of his eyes. It had been no dream.

She quickly leaned down to give Mena a reassuring hug and followed her maid back to the servants who awaited them in front of the cathedral.

They left the market behind, the crowds thinning as they moved closer to the Arno. Once over the famous Ponte Vecchio bridge, they turned towards a neighbourhood of grand *palazzi*, towards the Via Porcellatti. This was nothing like the terrible courtyard where she had become so lost—and then found.

It was quieter here, the shouts of the merchants and beggars behind them. There were still people, to be sure, many of them, going about their own business at a dignified, luxurious pace. Ladies in silken gowns and sheer veils anchored with jewelled bands emerged from the church of San Lorenzo as the bells tolled above them, trailed by their vigilant maids. Men in embroidered velvet doublets and sleeveless robes spoke together in hushed, intent voices, their gazes following her as she moved past. Servants scurried about on errands, heavy baskets over their arms. The shops were shaded with green awnings, offerings of gold, jewels and silks displayed to shining perfection.

The structures here were vast, solid, but built of plain, greyish-pink stone. Their heavy doors and lacy-screened balconies whispered of power, security, wealth. This was where the Strozzis lived.

Just as Caterina had directed in her letter, it was a perfect square of a *palazzo*, three storeys high, at the corner of a half-hidden square on the Via Porcellatti. In the distance, soaring high over the red-tiled roof, could be seen the ochre-coloured brick dome of the Duomo, Brunelleschi's famous achievement.

The shutters were half-open, offering shade in the warm afternoon, the doors closed and barred. But it was unmistakably their destination—the Strozzi arms hung over the portal.

'This must be it,' Mena murmured, her voice heavy with exhaustion. 'At last.'

Isabella glanced towards her maid. Mena's face was grey and drawn beneath her wide-brimmed straw hat, her eyes bloodshot. Their journey, such a rare source of pleasure and inspiration to Isabella until she was lost, had been only a trial to Mena. Had she been wrong to bring Mena with her? Or perhaps wrong to have come here herself? She should have been frightened, surely, but somehow she just felt—excited. She knew she could not leave now.

Isabella gave her a sympathetic smile. 'We *are* here, Mena! In no time at all we will have warm baths, good food and a clean bed to rest in.'

'Praise be to St Catherine!' Mena murmured fervently.

One of the footmen left his horse to bang the great brass ring against the heavy, iron-bound door. The sound reverberated through the courtyard within, echoing, and after only a moment they heard the inner bars being drawn back, the creak of hinges as the door opened to reveal a page clad in the embroidered Vespucci livery.

'The Signorina Isabella Spinola has arrived,' the footman said.

The page's gaze flickered past him, taking in Isabella and her ragged retinue. Surely, she thought, they were not an auspicious sight. She did not arrive in a silk-draped litter, followed by carts filled with clothes' chests and furniture. She had no large train of servants. And they were all covered in the dust and grit of the road, her plain, dark-blue-wool travel gown creased and dirty. She thought of the sheer veils and jewelled headdresses of the ladies they passed and reached up to touch her own hair. The thick, black length was simply braided and tucked into a net, covered by a flat velvet cap.

Doubt touched Isabella again. She was a country mouse, about to enter the palatial halls of the most sophisticated society in the world. What if her clothes, her manners, her *everything* were just wrong? So wrong Caterina laughed her out of the house, sending her back to where she started. Back to lonely ignorance. To men who were nothing like the angel in black she had met earlier.

But the page, rather than insisting she could not be Signorina Spinola and slamming the door, merely nodded. 'Of course. Signorina Strozzi is expecting you.'

He swung the door wider and several more liveried servants streamed out, hurrying down the steps to take their animals' bridles. 'They will take your horses around to the mews, Signorina Spinola. If you would care to follow me, the mistress has instructed me to take you to her at once.'

'Of course,' Isabella echoed, sliding down from her stiff Spanish saddle with the help of one of Caterina's servants. Her legs felt turned to ice water, unsteady beneath her. Once she stepped through those doors, she could not turn back. Could not run away.

Coward! her mind whispered. *What are you waiting for? Has this not been what you wanted for so very long? Your blood is as fine as hers, as ancient and noble. Don't shame your father—or yourself.*

Isabella stiffened her back, straightened her shoulders. She was no coward. She never had been. She just had to go forward, even if the stone facade of the *palazzo* contained the mouth of hell itself. There was no other choice. Not now. And surely she would have it no other way.

Her head tilted high, she followed the page through those doors. Only to find an earthly paradise, untouched by even a hint of fiery torment. Even the modern tumult of the city seemed leagues away.

Isabella stood still for a moment, gazing around in silent wonder. The courtyard was open to the sky, but the overhanging roof that covered the second-floor gallery gave shade and coolness. A tall marble fountain presided in the very centre, sparkling water spilling from a stone nymph's urn into a shimmering, bubbling stream. The pale pink flagstones were swept and scrubbed, lined with classical statues, gods, goddesses and heroes interspersed with backless benches and chairs that invited quiet conversation, solitary contemplation. It looked just like one of the etchings in her father's books, a Roman villa come to life.

How her father would have loved it.

'Signorina?' the page said softly.

Isabella glanced at him, startled. She had forgotten he was there, forgotten she was not alone in the midst of this perfect beauty. He smiled—obviously he was accustomed to such reactions.

'Shall I take you to Signorina Strozzi now?' he asked. 'She is most eager to greet you.'

'Of course,' Isabella murmured. *'Grazie.'*

She followed the page across the courtyard, past the rows of statues, whose blank stares seemed to follow her just as those of the men in the street had, judging her. At the far end rose a wide stone staircase, ascending in a soaring arc to the terrace. They were only halfway up these steps when a door at the top opened and a painting come to shining life stepped out.

It had to be Caterina. Isabella had not seen her kinswoman since she was a child, but she well remembered the occasion. She remembered how she, a dark, shy little girl, stood in awe of her older cousin, who seemed made of the rays of the sun, so beautiful and graceful was she. Everyone whispered that Caterina was destined for great things, for a place of fame and renown, and soon after that she seemed off to a fine start in her glorious life. Once she had even been betrothed to one of the Vespucci family, but rumours of her ill health had made that false.

Awe was a fine word for Isabella's emotions on that long-ago day. Awe that a human being could be so perfect, could be all that she herself was not. Fair, serene, accomplished, self-possessed. Awe and—and envy.

Those feelings hadn't changed with the years, Isabella found, as she stared up at her cousin. Caterina stood framed in the arched doorway, one of her statues come to life. Her skin was pale as marble, touched with pink only along the high, smooth cheekbones, the perfect foil for the loose fall of waving, red-gold hair that flowed to her waist. She wore an open robe of sky-blue silk over an even paler blue muslin gown, shades that matched her eyes. If Isabella were to paint her, she would use priceless blue marine.

Caterina gave a welcoming smile and hurried along the terrace. Her arms, draped in long, gold-lined sleeves, were outstretched in welcome.

'My dear cousin!' she cried, enveloping Isabella in a rose-scented embrace. 'You are here at last. Was your journey terribly taxing?'

Caterina was not very tall, yet still she was taller than Isabella, who had to go on tiptoe to kiss her smooth cheek. Caterina was all that was lovely, but Isabella found, as she returned the greeting embrace, that her cousin had grown thin, her shoulders all sharp-edged beneath her sumptuous robe. She felt warm, too, as if feverish and her blue eyes glowed with an unnatural light.

Once again, Isabella was sure she should conceal what had really happened to her on the journey. The danger *and* the rescue. 'Not at all,' she answered with a smile. 'We travelled in easy stages. I am very glad to be here, though. It was most kind of you to invite me.'

Caterina shrugged, still smiling as she stepped back, her eyes quickly taking in Isabella in a barely perceptible sweep. What could she think of her small, black-haired country cousin? She gave no indication, merely widened her smile, a dimple appearing in the alabaster of her cheek.

'What is family for, my dear Isabella? You have done me a great favour by leaving your home and coming to stay with me. This house will be less quiet and lonely with you here. But come, you must be hungry after your journey.

Paolo, will you fetch a repast for us and tell the maids we require a bath? And now, Isabella, you must tell me how your father fares. He was always one of my mother's favourite kinsmen. She constantly spoke of how learned and wise he is.'

The page—who must be Paolo—bowed and turned back down the stairs, as Caterina linked her arm with Isabella's and led her upwards. As Isabella assured Caterina that her father was well and still learned, they passed through that arched doorway into what surely must be Caterina's own rooms. They lacked the stiff formality of the public rooms of the house, the grand *sale*, the banquet halls and counting rooms. What they did not lack, though, was luxury.

The marble floors were covered with rare carpets, woven of glowing jewel shades of red and blue, while the walls were hung with tapestries depicting the wedding at Cana, and Diana at the hunt. Any thread of chill that might dare to creep through was banished by those rich, muffling threads. There was little furniture in this room, a few painted chairs and tables, and a lute and a set of virginals waiting in the corner.

Caterina led her through another doorway into the bedchamber, a sunlit expanse where the velvet curtains were drawn back from the leaded windows to let in vast, buttery swathes of light. The beams fell across the floor, covered with yet more rugs, along the immense carved bed on its raised platform. The mattress was draped in thickly embroidered blue-satin hangings and spread with a blue counterpane, but the bedclothes were rumpled, as if Caterina had only recently risen from their embrace. There were carved chests, upholstered chairs, polished-looking glasses and the sweet scent of smouldering herbs from the pierced brass globes suspended from the frescoed ceiling.

Isabella stared around her in amazement. A space more different from her whitewashed chamber at home could scarce be envisioned. 'I cannot imagine such a house ever being quiet,' she murmured.

Caterina laughed. 'I assure you it is! Such a vast, echoing space just for Matteo and me. That is why I go out so often. And why you will, too.' For an instant, a flicker of shadow passed over Caterina's face, a cloud on the bright sun. Then, it was gone and she smiled again.

'Let me show you your chamber, Isabella,' she said. 'I had it arranged just for you.'

The room was next to Caterina's, a smaller echo of it in furnishings and decorations. The bed was draped in dark rose-pink, as were the windows. Two carved chairs, a small table and an empty embroidery frame sat by the hearth and the clothes' chests were open, waiting to receive her possessions.

'It looks most comfortable,' Isabella said. 'I am sure I will be happy here.'

'*Va bene.* If you have need of anything, you have only to ask. I want you to feel this is your home, for as long as you care to stay.' Caterina strolled over to one wall, hung with tapestries woven with scenes of a Grecian banquet in soft creams and greens. Between them was a painting, not large, but exquisitely framed in gilt scrollwork. 'And this is one of my treasures. I thought you might enjoy it.'

Isabella drifted after her, completely mesmerized, drawn closer by the lure of the vibrant, unearthly colours. She had never seen anything like it in her life. The scene was a typical one, a Madonna with the infant Christ on her knee, set before a hazy, pale green-and-gold landscape. Isabella saw such subjects every day, in churches and country villas. She herself sketched visions of the Virgin. But never like this.

The blue and white of the Madonna's robe, her golden hair, the peachy warmth of her skin and that of her child—it glowed with pure, real life. As smooth as satin on its base, there was not a flaw to be seen. There was such an ineffable grace about the scene, an accuracy of line and a delicacy of feeling. The Virgin's outstretched hand was so fragile in its long grace, so beckoning, Isabella almost reached out to touch her. She curled her own fingers tightly in the folds of her skirt before she could do something so foolish.

Caterina studied the painting, too, her head tilted slightly in unconscious imitation of the Madonna.

'Is it not exquisite?' she said. 'It is by Giovanni Bellini of Venice, using the new method of mixing pigment with oil.'

'I have never seen anything so beautiful,' Isabella answered truthfully, vowing to herself to learn more of this new, magical technique.

Caterina smiled. 'I was told that you enjoy art, cousin. That you are a fine artist yourself.'

'I am no artist,' Isabella said. 'No true artist, like this Signor Bellini. I have had little training. But I do love art. Its beauty is the best of what it means to be human, is it not? It raises us—higher.'

Caterina gazed at her steadily, one golden brow arched, and Isabella felt her cheeks slowly heat. 'That is well said, Isabella. Art does indeed raise us above the daily struggle of our lives. It helps us to imagine what it might be like to touch divinity.' She reached out suddenly to clasp Isabella's hand. Her fingers were as dry and delicate as paper. 'I know our families have not always been the most harmonious, cousin, but I am so glad you are here now.'

And, suddenly, so was Isabella. Those silly doubts she had on the street were gone. The thieves, the gloriously handsome man who had rescued her—they just seemed part of the dream of the city. An adventure. She glanced back at the painting, that object of perfect, unattainable beauty that now seemed just the merest bit closer. 'I hope that I can be of some help to you.'

Caterina shook her head. 'You help me just by being here. We will be great friends, I am sure.'

The chamber door opened behind them, admitting a parade of servants bearing platters of food, ewers of wine and water, even a large wooden bathtub.

'At last!' Caterina said. 'You must be so famished by now.' She moved away from Isabella's side, becoming every inch the stern chatelaine as she supervised the servants in their pouring of the bath and serving of the food.

As Isabella turned back to the Bellini for one more glance, her attention was caught by yet another painting. This one hung by the open door, framed more simply but just as lovely. The colours were more muted than the Bellini, giving it an air of ethereal fancy. The subject was Caterina herself, depicted from just above her waist in a low-cut gown of pale pinkish-red. Her glorious hair was piled atop her head in loose waves, anchored with loops of a white scarf. She gazed off somewhere to her right, a half smile on her lips.

Around her neck was draped a heavy gold necklace, in the ominous shape of a serpent with ruby eyes. Was it a symbol of her mysterious illness, her withdrawal from the world?

Startled by the image, Isabella glanced back at her cousin, who was still overseeing the servants. Caterina was smiling, yet still Isabella fancied she saw that shadow lurking. She thought again of her rescuer and the darkness held deep in his sea-green eyes.

'Now, cousin, you must eat,' Caterina said, oblivious to any shadows at all. 'And then I shall loan you one of my own gowns. We have somewhere very important to go this afternoon.'

Somewhere important? Was she to be tossed into this strange new life already, feet-first into cold waters? Isabella's stomach tightened. 'Caterina, I think...'

Before she could finish her words, there was a noise from outside the luxurious chamber. The clatter of heavy booted footsteps, dogs barking, the deep rumble of masculine laughter. The door flew open and a golden giant of a man strode inside.

Isabella was sure this was Caterina's brother, her own cousin Matteo, for he had his sister's tawny hair. But where Caterina was pale and slight, he was tall and broad-shouldered, exuding an exuberant energy. He wore a plain dark doublet and tall, mud-splattered leather boots, his pack of dogs crowding close behind him as if he had just come in from hunting.

'This must be our fair cousin, arrived at last!' he said, his voice booming incongruously in the delicacy of his sister's chamber. 'Isabella, Caterina has been able to speak of nothing but your arrival for weeks. 'Tis good for her to have a companion at last.'

'And I am most pleased to be here,' Isabella answered, a bit flustered at his sudden arrival. She had only really glimpsed Matteo in the past; he was always a moving blur of laughter and raw energy. Today was no different. He was a large, sunny presence, seeming to take over the whole space.

He seized her hand and raised it to his lips, holding on to it tightly for a moment longer than she would have expected. He had the gift of making a woman, of making anyone, feel they were the one he most wanted to see at that moment. Isabella wondered how she would paint him. As Apollo, dragging the sun behind him? No, Hercules, conquering the world.

For some reason, she thought of her dark rescuer, the mysteries in his eyes. These two men seemed so different, but which would be more dangerous?

'And so pretty, too,' he whispered with a laugh. 'Florence needs more pretty ladies.'

'No teasing our poor cousin, Matteo,' Caterina said. 'I am taking her to Signor Botticelli's studio this afternoon, so she can meet our friends.'

'*Va bene*. Mayhap he will want to paint her, as he has you, sister.' Matteo threw himself down on a *chaise longue* and reached for the pitcher of wine. His dogs tussled at his feet as Caterina gave them a disapproving glance. 'We will find you a husband while we're here, shall we, Isabella? A rich *condottierre*, mayhap?'

Isabella laughed. She had long known marriage was not for her. Art was everything. A husband would surely only get in the way. 'I look not for a husband now,' she said. She would never repeat her parents' mistakes, the grief that came from loving too much.

'You cannot steal her away from me just yet,

Matteo, and give her as a prize to one of your friends,' Caterina said, reaching for a sweetmeat to nibble. 'There will be time for marriage later.'

'*Sì,*' Matteo muttered. He studied Isabella over the rim of his goblet with a strange glint in his eyes. She had the strangest sense that her cousin, for all his exuberant good humour and charm, was not entirely to be trusted. 'Later...'

'You saw the lady to her destination?' Orlando asked as his guardsmen came into the sitting room of his lodgings. He stared down at the street below his window. The bustling crowd moved past on their usual early evening errands, full market baskets over the arms of maidservants, courtesans tottering on their high-heeled pattens, gangs of young men with garish-striped hose and clanking swords.

They all went by as if it was merely an ordinary day. As if something hadn't cracked and shifted, changing beyond recognition.

'Nay, my lord, she found her party again and

rejoined them,' one of the guards said. 'She seemed safe with them.'

Orlando watched a lady in black drift past, like a ghost. Or a dream, like the young dark-eyed woman had been. 'You were not seen by them?'

The man snorted. 'If we have no wish to be seen, my lord, then we are not seen.'

Orlando gave a wry smile. He glanced back over his shoulder at the cluster of men hovering in his doorway. It was true—they were most adept at blending into any crowd, with their dark clothes and bearded faces. Neither handsome nor plain, too grand or too ragged. Perfect for his own purposes. That was why he employed them, to help him keep an eye on the shifting loyalties of Florence.

And, it seemed, to help him rescue fair maidens.

He reached for a bag of coins and tossed it to them. 'My thanks. You did a good deed for your souls today.'

The guardsman grinned, revealing cracked

teeth. "Twould take more than that to save *our* souls, my lord.'

Orlando had to laugh. His soul, too, was irreparably stained, beyond hope. Yet there had been something in that lady's eyes as she looked up at him, an openness, a light that seemed to pull him up…

'Is there anything else, my lord?' the guard asked. 'Shall we find out where the lady is dwelling? Or track down those thieves and finish them off?'

Orlando shook his head. 'The thieves will come to a bad end soon enough. And the lady is safe now.'

Especially safe from *him*. He found he did want to know where she was, far more than he should. That light in her eyes had been so fascinating. But he knew that would not be wise. He was much too intrigued with her after only one meeting. It should go no further.

He turned back to the window. 'I will send for you if you are needed again.'

They left in a scuffle of fading footsteps, the

metallic click of their swords and daggers, and Orlando was alone again.

The sudden fight in that quiet square had made his blood hot, made it sing through his veins as it once did when he was a high-tempered youth. Tavern brawls held little attraction for him now. Such fights were a waste of his energy when far more serious matters pressed in around them. But when he came upon those filthy villains circling the lost, frightened lady, the old Orlando had surged back to life and a fury such as he had rarely known of late came back upon him.

And those eyes of hers, the delicacy of her hand as he helped her to her feet, aroused a lust just as sudden and fierce. He had wanted to kiss her, hard and deep, feel her body against his, as the furious rush of life carried them away. The tremble of her fingers, the wary gratitude on her face, held him back. He had done a fair deed; he couldn't ruin it by scaring her all over again.

Now the anger and the desire had ebbed away,

leaving him cold again. But the memory of her wouldn't be erased from his mind. She wasn't beautiful, not really, not in a city full of golden courtesans, but there was something much more than beauty in her face. Something he wanted to read.

So, nay—he should *not* find out where she lived. He should not see her again, for the sake of her as well as himself.

There was a knock at the door and his hand automatically went to the hilt of the dagger at his waist. The guards would not return without his summons. 'Yes?'

The manservant who usually watched the door below came in with a low bow. He held out a sealed letter. 'A message from the convent of St Clare. You asked that any word from them be brought to you right away.'

Orlando nodded and reached for the letter to break the seal and hastily scan the neatly penned words. He half-feared every time he heard from the convent that something ill had befallen little Maria. An illness, an accident—

perhaps even a kidnapping if Matteo Strozzi discovered her existence. Little Maria was always in his thoughts, his plans.

But the message was only an account of Maria's progress since he last visited. Her lessons in music, languages and her religious instruction went on well. She was a quick, bright child, as well as a beauty. Just as her mother had once been.

Orlando carefully refolded the letter. His sister's dark despair, her terrible love for a villain who was nowhere near worthy of her shining spirit, had taken her away from her daughter. Maria Lorenza would never hear her child's laughter, see her run through the sunshine. Everyone had betrayed her in the end.

Orlando would not.

And he could not afford to be turned from his avowed duty by maidens in distress—no matter how very intriguing they were.

Chapter Three

The sun was a richer golden colour, almost amber, when Isabella and Caterina left the Strozzi *palazzo*. The afternoon was on the wane, the siesta of the city just breaking. Shops were opening again, people emerging from their homes to seek out food for supper, amusement for the evening. Young men in bright, fashionable garments and elaborately plumed caps still lounged on the street corners, yet Isabella noticed that they did not stare so insolently as Caterina drifted by. Rather, these noisy youths watched her with wide eyes and mouths agape, as if a goddess suddenly floated into their prosaic midst. The danger she had faced earlier seemed absurdly far away.

And, though she looked most carefully, she did not see the man who had saved her in that deserted courtyard. She began to wonder if he had been a mere dream after all. If this glittering surface was all there really was to the city after all.

Caterina wore blue again, a narrowly cut gown of deep-sapphire velvet slashed with white satin, the sleeves tied with fluttering gold-and-silver ribbons. She sported no jewels, no sparkling diamonds or soft gleam of pearls to compete with the glow of her skin and eyes.

She had loaned Isabella a gown of bronze-coloured silk, trimmed with red ribbons and embroidery on the high-waisted bodice. It was a beautiful garment, crafted in the very latest style, yet still Isabella felt like nothing so much as a country mouse, clad in city finery that fooled no one. She almost laughed aloud at this hazy unreality, the dreamlike state of it all.

Caterina linked her arm with Isabella's, drawing her closer as they made their dignified progress along the street. 'It is not far now, cousin.

I go here every day. Sometimes I do not even return home until long after dark.'

Isabella was mystified. Caterina had told her nothing of their destination, merely shaking her head with a small smile on her lips when asked. Was it some very fine shop, a cathedral or gallery? Isabella was not at all sure she cared for this uncertainty, not on top of everything else that was so odd about this day. 'Caterina, will you not tell me where we are going?' she tried asking again.

'I told you, it is a surprise. But I promise you, Isabella, that you will like it very much indeed.'

They finally stopped before a building, much like the Strozzi house in size and solid stone structure. The outer windows were shuttered and there were no signs or coat of arms to indicate what lay inside.

One of Caterina's pages raised the brass door ring, bringing it down on the stout wooden door. After only a moment, the portal swung open.

Rather than another liveried servant, there

stood a young man in a paint-stained smock, a smear of dark charcoal along one cheek. He blinked for a second in the fading sunlight, as if startled by the day, before a wide, delighted smile spread across his face.

'Signorina Strozzi!' he cried happily. 'You are here. We have been wondering what was keeping you away this day.'

'Only the happiest of events, Jacopo,' Caterina answered. 'My cousin, Signorina Spinola, has come to stay with me. She is another great lover of art.'

'The master will be so very pleased.' The young man swung the door open wider and Caterina led them through. Rather than an open, classical courtyard, as at the Strozzi *palazzo*, they stepped into utter chaos.

But chaos of the most wondrous sort. The sort Isabella so often lay awake at night fantasising about. Longing for. The chaos of an artist's studio.

The high ceiling was enclosed in a thick glass skylight, pouring down sunshine on the activity below. Paintings were stacked along the walls, propped on easels, in all stages of readiness from just barely gessoed to completed scenes. People in stained smocks clustered around them, as bees in a summer hive, wielding bright brushes, arguing. The smell of turpentine and tempera paint was thick in her nostrils, heavy and acrid, as welcome as sweet springtime flowers.

As Isabella stared around her, enraptured, she felt Caterina's gentle touch on her arm. 'Well, cousin? What think you?'

Isabella smiled at her. 'I think it is perfection.'

Caterina laughed. 'And so it is! The very centre of all that is great in Florence. Come—we will meet the creator of this perfection.' She made her way through the swirling activity, still full of that gentle serenity even as greetings were called out to her, bows were made. She waved to them all, asking quick questions as they passed by. It was obvious that she came here very often, just as she had said. All these people knew her well.

And it gave Isabella a new wild, welling hope. Perhaps—oh, just perhaps—they could come to this glorious place every day. Then she could observe this work, learn from their techniques, make enquiries. If she could...

They followed the doorkeeper—Jacopo—through a high, arched doorway into a smaller, light-filled space. The flurry of motion was less here, the mingled conversation and cacophony less confused. For an instant, Isabella was captured by the images hung on the plain white walls and she could see, *feel* them, only them. There was a Judith, her maidservant behind her bearing the head of Holofernes; an Adoration of the Magi, the figures triangulated around the holy manger; a figure of Victory, clad in gleaming breastplate and helmet.

All typical scenes, of course, yet Isabella had never seen them executed in quite such a way. Every inch was suffused with a cool, graceful sensuality.

Isabella leaned closer to the Judith, studying the faint, painted smile of her coral-hued lips.

What thoughts did she conceal, this tranquil woman, after she had just sliced a man's head off with nary a drop of blood on her ice-blue gown? There was nary a ripple in her smile.

'Isabella!' Caterina called. 'Come, you must meet my dearest friend in all the world.'

Isabella reluctantly turned away from the painting to find her cousin standing a few feet behind her, her hand on the arm of a tall man in yet another paint-splashed smock. Yet Isabella could tell, with just one glance, that this man was not as those scurrying assistants, those worker bees, in the outer room.

He was very tall, broad-shouldered, with curling, dark-blond hair tumbling over his brow. He had a long, straight nose and high cheekbones in a bronzed face, sharply etched and clean-shaven. His eyes, a dark blue, glowed and burned with an inner fire, an undeniable force of life.

'This is Signor Botticelli, the finest artist in all of Florence,' Caterina said. 'Alessandro, this is my kinswoman, Isabella Spinola, who has been kind enough to come and stay with me. She, too, is a great lover of art.'

'Signorina Spinola! An honour to meet you. Florence has need of more cultured ladies of Caterina's ilk.' He reached for Isabella's hand, bowing over it with a courtly flourish. Isabella saw that his skin was stained with smears of priceless aquamarine, a trace of gilt glitter.

'And I am greatly honoured to make your acquaintance, Signor Botticelli,' she answered, her voice tight in her throat. 'One hears of your great work even in the countryside, though I never dreamed I could see it for myself.'

'That is gratifying indeed. Tell me, then, what do you think, now that you *have* seen it? Do you think our dear Caterina is correct and I am the finest artist in Florence?'

Isabella glanced back towards the Judith, the tangle of her golden hair, the twists of her flowing gown, the muted colours that somehow only made her seem more alive. 'I have not yet met all the artists of Florence. But I would say you are assuredly at the top of the competition.'

Botticelli threw back his head and laughed, a raucous noise that soared to the very skylights. Caterina laughed as well, a silvery sound that blended with his in a sweet music of merriment. Isabella couldn't help but smile, too.

'Well, once you have met all the artists, as I am sure you will do under your cousin's auspices, you must come back and give me your opinion, my dear Signorina Spinola. Now, would you care to see what I am working on? It is quite glorious, unsurpassed. Sure to be my masterpiece.'

His masterpiece—greater even than those transcendent works she had already seen? Isabella feared she might not be able to look on it without being blinded, but she only nodded. 'I would be honoured.'

Signor Botticelli took her arm in his solid clasp and turned her towards a large panel, hidden behind draperies of stained linen. His touch was alive with strength, crackling with barely suppressed energy and enthusiasm, and Isabella felt herself tremble in aching anticipation.

What beauty could possibly be hidden there, what unimaginable 'glories'?

Yet she was not to glimpse them. Not yet. Even as Signor Botticelli reached for the edge of the linen, even as Isabella held her breath, heart pounding, the studio doors burst open. For an instant, she thought it was that galloping heart, breaking free. Light and wind swept in, as fleet as if Jupiter himself drove the elements along. Startled, Isabella spun around, her unaccustomed narrow silk skirts wrapping around her legs—only to find that her fancies about gods come to Earth had not been far off. Surely these *were* gods, borne into the mortal world on golden chariots.

There were at least nine or ten men, a blur of bright velvets and plumed hats, gems and gold and sparkle, a tangle of energy and sheer glamour such as Isabella had never known, or even imagined. There were no men such as this in the country, only sages and beardless boys, rough farmers—careless scholars. Combined with the new force of the art, it was dizzying. Disorientating.

At their head was a tall, slender young man clad in a brilliant emerald-green doublet slashed with cloth of gold, trimmed with gold ribbons. His long, strong legs were set off by gold-and-green, parti-coloured hose, culminating in the most elaborate, most giggle-inducing codpiece she had ever seen. She nearly laughed aloud—was it shaped like a *boat*?—but her snicker caught in her throat when he swept off his cap and a tumble of glossy, dark-brown curls spilled to his broad shoulders. If ever someone could be said to be the masculine equal of Caterina in beauty, this was surely he. A perfect young godling, his perfect face alight with sparkling laughter.

'My beauteous Caterina!' he called, bowing low with a graceful flourish of his cap. The gilded plume swept the flagstone floor. 'I did hope I would find you here.'

Caterina smiled her mysterious, tranquil smile, yet Isabella glimpsed something behind that cool grace, that perfect stillness. A gleam in her blue eyes, a tremble of her fingers. 'You can scarce be surprised, Giuliano. I come here every day—as do you.'

'Ah, but we called at your house already and your servants told us they had no idea where you had gone. We were prepared to comb every street in Florence for you, if need be.'

The godling glanced over his shoulder to his companions, as if to elicit their agreements. They chorused their assent, bowing in a swirl of colour and shine. Could such a sight ever be captured in paint, such an unnatural rainbow? Isabella noticed that all the assistants, too, clustered in the doorway, watching in avid, awed silence. And who could ever blame them? It was not every day a fantasy burst into real life. Isabella found herself utterly bemused, a nigh permanent state since she rode through the Gate of Fortune into this magic city.

'And what was of such vast import, my lord, that you had to rush about in such a state to find me?' Caterina said, her voice edged with teasing laughter. 'Surely we will meet tomorrow, if not here, then at the festival.'

'Not soon enough.' He stepped closer, the bells on his green velvet shoes singing, and took up Caterina's hand, pressing a soft kiss to her very fingertips. Those fingers did not tremble now. 'We have come to solicit your approval for a new scheme.'

'A new scheme?' Caterina gave him a tender smile, her eyes half-closed, but her hand she gently withdrew from his clasp. 'What is it this time? Nay, wait, before you tell me, you must meet my cousin. I shall want to hear *her* thoughts on your—scheme.'

Caterina turned away from him with a soft whisper of her gown, her gaze searching out Isabella. Thus Isabella found herself drawn from her world of semi-shadows, silent observation, upwards towards the sun. With no wings at all. 'Isabella Spinola is my kinswoman, who has come to Florence to be my dear friend,' Caterina said, taking Isabella's hand in hers. Caterina's skin was cold.

Up close, the god was even more intimidating than at a safe distance. His flesh was perfectly smooth, touched with a faint golden cast; his dark eyes sparked and deflected, like black ice in winter.

They surveyed Isabella closely, yet gave no hint of a reaction in return.

'And this, Isabella,' Caterina said, still that faint mischief, that tease, in her tone, 'is the most amusing clown in all Florence. Giuliano de Medici.'

'Alas, Caterina, you wound me!' Giuliano clasped his hand over his heart, stumbling back a step as if pierced by an arrow tip. 'You will give your fair cousin the wrong idea of me. I assure you, Signorina Spinola—it *is signorina*, is it not?—that I am only ever your kinswoman's most devoted servant. I "clown" only to see her smile.'

'And obviously you do succeed, Signor Giuliano,' Isabella assured him. 'You see how she smiles now, yet seeks to hide it?'

'I dare say you are right!' Giuliano exclaimed.

'I definitely see a dimple, just there. So, I cannot be so useless as all that.'

An edge of bitterness had crept into his charming laughter, but Caterina merely flicked her pale jewelled hand at him, as if in dismissal. 'I never said you were *useless*. No man who writes such fine poetry could ever be of no use to a lady. Do you not agree, Isabella?'

'Indeed,' Isabella assured hastily. 'Why, you are spoken of even in my home in the country, *signor*. Your fame is so very great.' And that was true. Her father's visiting scholar friends *did* speak of this younger Medici, the brother or Lorenzo, *Il Magnifico*, yet what they said spoke of his love of fashion, art—and beautiful women. Of how he seemed to take no part of the business and commerce of the city, of his family's banking interests.

Her words seemed to please him, though; for he laughed and said, 'I think I shall like this cousin of yours, Caterina!'

'That is very well, for she is going to stay with me for a long time to come,' Caterina answered. 'And you will find her here with me every day, as she loves art as I do.'

'Indeed?' Giuliano said, a spark of interest in those black-ice eyes. 'Surely I would have expected no less from any relative of Caterina. Tell me, Signorina Spinola, what do you think of our Botticelli's work?'

Isabella hesitated, glancing over her shoulder to find Signor Botticelli standing near one of his easels, his muscled arms crossed over his paint-splashed chest. He watched their group carefully, gauging, weighing, as if they were mere objects to be committed to canvas or panel. A sum of parts—arms, legs, hair, eyes, ready to be transformed into a translucent Madonna, a goddess, a spirit, a tortured saint.

A wave of shyness struck Isabella, almost nauseating in its chill. Who was *she* to speak of this art in front of *them*? How could she even find words to stammer out? All she had were emotions, overwhelming feelings and longings. Longings that came out so strongly when she thought of her green-eyed rescuer.

Her eyes suddenly prickled behind her lashes and she feared she might cry.

Fool! she thought fiercely. *Fool. Not here, not now.*

Caterina seemed to sense her distress, or something of it, for she took Isabella's hand in hers and said, 'How can she say, when she has scarcely even seen Alessandro's work? He was about to show her his new scene, when you came bursting in like some wild bravos. Why don't we walk over there while Isabella examines the paintings and you can tell me your great secret?'

Giuliano led Caterina away, his friends tumbling behind them. Isabella was glad of the sudden quiet, the space that opened up around her. She wandered in the other direction, away from the echo of laughter. She took in the canvases stacked along the walls, the swirl of colour and beauty that was almost too much to bear. She found herself behind a screen, with a table laid out before her that was grander than any banquet.

Clear jars and pots held chunks of minerals, swirls of dyes—ochre, greenish-brown under-washes, vermilion, purple, priceless lapis, even flakes of pure, shining gold. All waiting there, just for her, like a box of jewels.

As she drew closer, her breath held, she saw the piles of brushes in all sizes, the charcoal sticks and planes of poplar for stretching canvases. Everything an artist could want, everything so hard to find in her country home, all in one place. It was amazing.

Isabella leaned over a selection of valuable crushed-insect pigments, envisioning the sheer veil on Signor Botticelli's painting. What could be used to create such an effect?

'You are an artist, then, *signorina*?' a deep, quiet voice said behind her.

Isabella gasped and spun around, half expecting to see one of the artist's assistants come to demand how she, a mere female, could be caught snooping about. Her mouth opened to explain herself, but the words suddenly strangled in her throat. The man before her was not like any of the pale young apprentices she had seen running around the studio.

If he *was* a man and not an angel. For there he was again, the man who had saved her from the thieves the day she arrived. And she had begun to think he must have been a figment of her imagination!

But, no. He was as beautiful as she remembered, transcendentally so, but she saw right away the comparison to an angel was not apt. The darkness that she had glimpsed when he fought the thieves, the darkness that had frightened and thrilled her in equal measure, was still there.

He looked like a Hades, sailing the dusky waters of the Styx towards his shadowy kingdom. He was tall and lean, with dark brown curls brushed back from the perfectly sculpted, almost harsh angles of his face. His eyes, green and unreadable, stared down at her, but reflected nothing back. She was used to reading people as she sketched them, trying to find the essence of them to give life to her paintings, but this man was completely baffling.

Unlike Giuliano de Medici and his merry band of friends, this man again wore black. A black-velvet doublet, narrow-sleeved and high-necked, trimmed with the moonlight glint of silver. Black hose, soft black boots. An onyx set in silver dangled from his ear, tangling with those dark curls.

Was he really a mirage, a spirit come to drag her down to the afterlife? Hades, that was surely who he was, the dark king of the underworld.

But then he smiled at her and she knew he was no illusion. He was all too real.

'We have met before, *signor*,' she said hoarsely. 'You did me a great service.'

'I did only what any gentleman would have done for a lady. Forgive me, *signorina*, but I thought I knew all the artists in Florence,' he said, giving her a small half smile that only seemed to increase his beauty and mystery. 'Only an artist could look so enthralled by brushes.'

'What makes you think I am an artist?' Isabella said, intrigued. 'I could be an artist's assistant, sent on an errand for pigments and brushes.'

'A most devoted servant, then.' He gestured towards her hand, the charcoal streaks on her skin that could never completely wash away.

She laughed ruefully and tucked her hand into the folds of her skirt. The dark avenger of their first meeting was gone and now he was all light banter. Her head spun with confusion. 'I'm an amateur only, *signor*, though I hope to learn more while I'm here.'

'And what is it you wish to learn? Better things than what greeted your arrival, I hope.' He leaned on the edge of the screen, his arms crossed carelessly over his chest. He watched her closely, seemingly truly curious.

It made her feel uncomfortable—that steady gaze of his from such endlessly green eyes made her feel like she couldn't quite catch her breath. She looked away, back to the array of brushes, but she could still feel him watching her.

What was it she wanted to learn? *Everything,* she wanted to cry out. Everything Signor Botticelli knew, so she could capture this man's beauty on canvas and never lose it.

'I wish to—to—' she said, then broke off, suddenly dizzy. Dizzy from the whirl of sights and smells, from this man's intoxicating presence. He had only said a few words to her, yet she was alarmingly fascinated. She pressed her hand to her spinning head.

'Are you weary from your journey to Florence?' he asked, all his teasing and smiles gone. He made a movement towards her, so close she could smell the light, warm scent of his citrus cologne. She instinctively took a step back and he stopped.

'I was weary when my cousin insisted we come here,' she answered, glancing at him from the corner of her eye. That seemed like the only safe way to watch him. 'It's a long journey and I'm not quite accustomed to riding such distances. And—well, you know what happened when I arrived. But somehow, when

I came through the gates of Florence and saw everything that was here, that weariness was gone. It's all so astonishing, not like anything at home.'

She had no idea why she would confide in him, a stranger, like that. Unless he really could cast enchanted spells. But he just smiled at her, so gentle. 'Truly, *signorina*, there is no time to be weary in Florence.'

'None at all.' Isabella laughed and had the sudden, insane urge to twirl around and around, to take in everything, every *palazzo*, every fountain, every person, and hug them close to her. Especially this man. This man, with his unfathomable gaze and the dark beauty that was unlike anything she had ever seen before. 'To sleep would mean to miss something! Surely there's more here than could be seen in one lifetime.'

He laughed, a deep, dark chuckle that made her think of fires on cold winter nights. Of spiced wine and all warm, summer-bright things, despite his black attire. 'You have decided all that already, *signorina*? Most people *do* take a lifetime to absorb even one tiny ounce of this city. Of what it all means.'

'It's true that I have a great deal to learn. But I think I've now seen the greatest sight in all Florence,' she said, feeling the strangest urge to tease him a bit. To make him laugh again.

He tilted his head as he watched her curiously. 'The Ponte Vecchio? The dome of the cathedral?'

'Nay, though I'm sure those are beautiful. I've seen something everyone, especially ladies, would appreciate.'

His dark brow arched. 'Is that so?'

'Yes. I have seen a real artist's studio, where beauty is created.' Or where beauty, like his own, was merely reflected.

He did laugh again and she had to laugh with him. 'Then I was right. You are an artist.'

'Not a true artist. Just a dabbler.' Isabella thought of the paintings on Caterina's walls. 'I don't have the elevated tastes some possess. But I do love art. It's been my friend for as long as I can remember. Colour, line, shape—they dance in my mind and won't leave me alone.'

Her laugh turned nervous as she realized she was confiding her deepest self to this Hades. There was something in his eyes that seemed to draw it out of her. She turned away again, studying the pigments in their jars. 'You must think me addled, *signor*. I fear I have little courtly polish yet.'

'I hope you may never gain it, then, fair *signorina*,' he said suddenly, intensely. She glanced back to him, startled, to see his eyes were very dark. 'Florence is filled with polished ladies, as hard as diamonds. Ladies who always guard their thoughts. Who laugh so carefully, and sigh, and never speak of what they truly love. What they really find vital in life.'

'And art is vital,' she murmured, captivated by his sudden passionate words.

'Everyone here speaks of art, buys and sells it, but who really feels its essence deep in their souls? Who sees that it's more than mere fashion, more than a superficial beauty? More than base politics.'

'Yes. It is life,' Isabella whispered. Life— what she saw now in his eyes, sparkling and fizzing as a fine wine.

'Exactly. And you can see it here, if you look deep enough.'

She felt something tug deep inside of her, a shimmering, unknown filament that connected her to this stranger. 'I do think that—'

'Isabella!' Caterina suddenly called, just beyond the screen. 'Where are you? We must return home soon!'

'Coming, Caterina!' she called, instinctively turning towards the sound. When she turned back around, her Hades was gone, vanished as if he had never been there at all. She almost thought she had imagined him, yet a faint trace of citrus cologne hung in the warm air.

Who was he? Would she ever see him again?

'Coming, Caterina,' she called again. As she left her haven behind the screen, she felt like Lot's wife, her entire being straining to look back, to find that man again, to talk to him more. But there was only the real-life world, the crowded room of swirling colours and hurrying assistants. Paradise closed to her. But surely she would find him again? Surely Caterina would know who he was?

Clinging to that thought, she hurried to join her cousin and all of Caterina's laughing, jostling friends.

Orlando stood hidden in the window embrasure, watching the lady hurry away. A veil was drawn over her glossy dark hair, concealing most of her profile from him, but he remembered exactly how she looked. The light of wonder in her wide eyes. The soft hesitation of her smile, which when it came made it seem like the sun had emerged. He had to know who she was, where she had come from, for surely it was from a different world than the hidden darkness of Florence. He had not been able to think of anything but her since they parted in that courtyard.

There was a flurry of movement in the studio behind him, the quick whiff of paint, and Signor Botticelli appeared beside Orlando to peer down at the street.

'A most interesting young lady,' Botticelli said musingly. 'She seems most appreciative of art.'

Orlando laughed wryly. She had indeed seemed appreciative. More than that, awestruck. 'Who in Florence does not appreciate art, my friend? They keep you very busy, decorating their chapels and *palazzi.*'

Botticelli shrugged. 'To impress their friends. But a true love of beauty…'

Orlando remembered how the dark-haired lady had studied the array of brushes and tools with a rapt absorption most Florentine women gave to velvets and ribbons. She was truly intriguing. 'Is rare.'

'And she is a beauty herself,' Botticelli said. 'Of a most unusual sort. I'd like to paint her. Mayhap as Artemis of the hunt. Perhaps she will return here soon. Shall I send you word if she does come back, Signor Landucci?'

Orlando glanced up to find the artist smiling at him and he suddenly felt like a schoolboy being teased for an unrequited passion. 'Why should you do that?'

'You liked her, did you not? I haven't seen you look at a lady thus since the brightest days of the fair Lucretia.'

Orlando stared back down at the street. His dark-haired lady was long gone, swallowed up in the crowds of market-goers with their baskets on their arms, servants bearing bundles and bolts of fabric, bravos looking for trouble, monks in their robes. She was no longer there, but he could still see her in his mind so clearly. Her glossy sable hair, her eyes so wide and shining with delight as she turned around and around, taking in all the beauty around her as if she would absorb it and make it part of herself.

He had lived so long amid the cynicism of Florence, the watchful stares, the whispered

gossip and family quarrels, that her wonder
had swept over him like the sweetest of summer breezes, clearing away the ugliness of everyday life.

He wanted to talk to her more, look at her
and see if her sun-touched skin was as soft as
it looked.

'As you said,' he murmured, 'she is pretty in
a most unusual way. You should paint her as a
forest nymph.'

'A most excellent idea,' Botticelli said. 'Dark
and mysterious, dwelling in the shadows of the
trees. And shall I tell you when she comes back
here to model for me?'

Orlando turned his back on the life of the
street, his arms crossed over his chest. 'You
can start by telling me her name and what she
is doing here in Florence.'

'Her name is Isabella,' Botticelli said. 'Cousin
to the beauteous Caterina Strozzi, who was
here with her.'

Strozzi. Orlando stiffened, all fanciful, flirtatious thoughts swept away by a sudden chill. 'Cousin to Matteo Strozzi.'

Botticelli, who knew nothing of what had happened in Orlando's past with the Strozzi family, shrugged. 'She must be, though I care naught for Signor Matteo. Unlike his lovely sister, he has no care for culture or beauty. Let us hope Signorina Spinoli resembles her cousin Caterina.'

Orlando knew that the girl could have nothing to do with Strozzi's foul deeds. She had only just come to Florence and her eyes shimmered with her innocence. The innocence that had led her into such trouble when he first encountered her. Yet she *was* related to Matteo, she was his family, and in Florence that made her Orlando's enemy.

Yet he still wanted to see her, Isabella, again. Far more than he dared admit, even to himself. He was damned no matter what he did.

Chapter Four

The cloth over the painting was about to be drawn back. Isabella could see the edge of the linen flutter, as enticing as the jewelled edge of a woman's veil, and her heart pounded in anticipation. She couldn't breathe, couldn't move. Something momentous was about to be revealed. It felt as if she stood poised before the throne of heaven, all truths about to be revealed, all beauties and joys. Soon she would possess them herself, and her wild thoughts would be over.

The cloth gusted as if in a great winter breeze, showing her a glimpse of bright colours—yellow, green, white, vivid blue, hot red. Then the curtain fell still again. Why was it all suddenly

*so far away? It had been so close! She might
have reached out and snatched the veil away
once and for all. But now the floor under her
feet, cold, grey-tinged marble, stretched out
under her, moving her away from what she
sought so desperately.*

*Isabella lifted the heavy hem of her skirts,
running, slipping, only to find that her prize
was farther away than ever. Her shoes stuck to
the marble, a hobble at her ankles. Her gown,
a fine, heavy robe of silver brocade, grew even
weightier.*

*All around her rose a chorus of whispers.
Soft at first, enticing as a summer breeze, they
grew louder and louder until they roared and
screamed. Tearing at her ears. But she could
hear no words, no sense. Men's voices, wom-
en's, the wail of an infant.*

*She tried to cover her ears, but she couldn't
lift her hands. The veiled painting was a mere
speck at the end of the ice chamber.*

*Suddenly her skirts freed her and she ran, ran
as fast as she could from the whispers and the*

roaring wind. It caught on the linen and blew it away from the painting at last.

'No!' she screamed. She stumbled and fell, but still she couldn't look away from what was revealed. Not the beauty she expected, but a Minotaur, half bull, half man, hulking, black, with glowing red eyes. As Isabella watched, horrified, one clawed paw swooped out and the Minotaur was charging towards her across the room, trailing flames in its wake.

But its face—its face was beautiful. The face of her unknown Hades...

'Nay!' Isabella cried, sitting straight up in her borrowed bed. For an instant, she didn't know where she was, what was happening to her. That clawed hand still reached for her. She shuddered deeply, her whole body shaking, as she rubbed her cold hands over her eyes.

She drew in a deep breath, then another, until the buzzing whispers in her head slowed, stilled, and she became aware of her true surroundings again.

She wasn't in some ice chamber. There were

no flames surrounding her. She was in her luxurious new chamber, tucked in the middle of a palatial bed, the hangings of dark-blue brocade drawn around her. The covers were tossed and twisted, the bolsters buried under the tangle of linen and velvet. She had had a bad dream again, like the dreams that had plagued her when she was a child and had missed her mother. What could have brought it on now?

She laughed, still shaking. It was only a dream, probably brought on by what happened when she arrived in Florence. Those terrifying moments before Hades had come to her rescue—only to send her spinning into more confusion when he appeared again. She had vowed never to love anyone as her father had loved her mother. It only led to grief. Grief and bad dreams.

'*Signorina?*' someone called, making Isabella jump, startled. But it was only Mena, drawing back the bed curtains. Sturdy, steady Mena, already dressed for the day in her grey gown and white cap. The curtains were looped back from the windows, letting in the greyish-pink light of the Florentine predawn.

'*Signorina*, are you well?' Mena said, her brow creased with worry. 'You cried out. Did you have another bad dream? Like when you were a child?'

She did not want to admit the truth to Mena that her childhood dreams had returned. 'It's always difficult to adjust to a new bed, I suppose. I'll be more restful tonight. How was your own sleep, Mena?'

Mena gave a disdainful snort as she straightened the twisted bedclothes. 'These Florentine servants! How they chatter, like magpies. I could hardly find a moment's peace.'

'Maybe you would rather sleep in here. There's a truckle bed…'

'And be awakened at all hours by your dreams? I would rather not, Signorina Isabella.' She plumped the bolsters. 'What was it this time?'

Isabella turned away. She didn't want to talk about it. The cold marble room, the whispers, the monster with her handsome Hades's face. It all seemed so silly now, yet it had been so frightening. 'I told you, Mena. Just this strange bed.'

'Humph.' Mena didn't seem convinced, but she said nothing more. She laid a tray over Isabella's lap. 'Eat your bread and ale. The food in this house is so rich, so full of spices. You need something simple and nourishing.'

Isabella laughed. Mena really was dear to her. 'I know you think we should have stayed at home, Mena, but I promise you all will be well here, once we're accustomed to it.'

'My lamb.' Mena gently smoothed the tangles of Isabella's hair, as she had when Isabella was a mere child and she'd had a bad dream. 'I know there was nothing for you at your father's house. But I can't help but fear for you here. These people...'

Isabella shivered again as she thought of her mysterious Hades. 'What do you mean?'

Mena shook her head. 'Servants always talk too much, my lamb. It is just gossip. But you should always be careful. This isn't a simple place. There are so many feuds and romances, so many....'

Feuds and romances, alliances, secrets. 'Like a maze.'

Mena frowned. 'A maze?'

'I won't get lost, Mena,' Isabella said, thinking of the Minotaur monster. 'I have a ball of twine.'

'Oh, lamb!' Mena said with a laugh. 'The things you say. You are your father's daughter.'

'Am I?' Everyone had always said she looked like her lost mother. It was something she clung to, but also feared.

'Eat your bread. You need your strength. You are too thin.'

''Tis fashionable to be thin here.' Isabella chewed a nibble of bread as she watched Mena fold clothes into the carved chest. As she reached for her goblet of ale, the door opened and a maidservant bustled in with another borrowed gown over her arm.

'Good morning, *signorina*,' she said, bobbing a curtsy. 'I have a message from Signorina Caterina.'

'I hope my cousin is well this morning,' Isabella said, finishing her bread.

'Very well, *signorina*, but she begs your pardon. She has a headache and cannot yet rise from her bed. She will see you at dinner this evening. Signor Matteo has already gone for the day.'

Isabella frowned as she remembered her cousin's frail look, her tired eyes before she retired after they returned from Signor Botticelli's. 'Should I not go to her?'

The maid shook her head, the gown she held rustling. 'These headaches usually pass. The mistress said you should not postpone any of your pleasures today. She will be well later. And she sends this gown for you. The cloth merchants and dressmakers will wait on you tomorrow.'

'*Grazie*. Tell Caterina I will see her soon,' Isabella said.

Mena took the garments from the girl and shooed her out the door, closing it behind her.

'Well, Mena,' Isabella murmured. 'What do you think of all this?'

Mena smoothed out the new gown, an elaborate creation of blue-and-cream taffeta stripes with gold braid and slashed sleeves. 'I think you should be careful not to get into trouble, with such gowns and a whole day to yourself.'

Isabella laughed. She knew of only one thing that drove away doubts and fears—work. 'How well you know me. I do have an errand in mind for today…'

Chapter Five

'*Pesce*! *Pesce*! The freshest fish in all Florence, only caught this very morning...'

'Ribbons, *signorina*! The finest silk ribbons in the *mercato*. A scarlet one, mayhap, for your beautiful black hair?'

'Nay, *signorina*, do not listen to him! *These* are the finest ribbons to be had. Blue, green, threads of gold...'

Isabella laughed and shook her head at the cries of the duelling merchants. They had seemed everywhere in the city ever since she arrived. She waved them off and continued on her way, alone. She had left Caterina's bored pageboy, who was meant to be her escort, watching his friends play at dice so she could go about her errand unencumbered. She couldn't be distracted now by baubles and ornaments, even though she was coming to see those would have to be a concern of hers here in Florence. Today she had a more important goal in mind and little time for it. Soon Caterina would leave her chamber and be asking for her.

Isabella thought about her fitful sleep last night. Her dream that had been interrupted by visions of her handsome Hades. She wondered now who he was, where he was and if she would soon see him again. And she didn't want to be so distracted. Not when romance seemed so fraught with hidden meanings and perils here in the city.

The Mercato Vecchio was crowded with drapers' tables spread with bolts of bright silks; bakers with glistening loaves of fresh bread and sugar-dusted cakes; pyramids of fresh fruits and vegetables newly brought in from the countryside. Booksellers, candle makers, purveyors of second-hand clothes, all added their voices to the clamour, with the counter-notes of maidservants and footmen. Everything was fresh and new so early in the morning.

Isabella dodged her way through the bright maze, her goal now in sight. A canopied booth tucked behind the fluttering colours of a feather merchant. The crowded counter seemed to beckon her.

Mayhap she didn't know the labyrinthine ways of Florence. Perhaps she couldn't yet understand the heavy, secret yearnings Hades had awakened in her when he smiled at her. But this she knew. This made her feel strong again.

As she drew closer, she glimpsed piles of brushes in all sizes, charcoal sticks in their boxes. Clear glass jars held chunks of minerals and swirls of dye. Everything an artist could want, all the things she found so hard to obtain in the country, all here in one place.

She saw there were a few other patrons in the booth already, young artists' apprentices with stained smocks and charcoaled hands, and the proprietor was yet too busy to pay her any mind. She felt the light weight of her purse at her belt and knew she had to carefully consider her purchases today.

She inspected a solution of crushed-insect pigments, which could create rich, dark colours. Dark enough for her Hades's hair, a glossy sable blackness against Persephone's silvery brightness as he caught her in his arms…

Nay. She shook her head, trying to banish the thought of him again. They had only met for a few moments, spoken a handful of words. Why should she think of him now?

Yet she feared she knew why she thought of him. Because he held a dangerous fascination within him she couldn't seem to forget.

Isabella ran her fingertips over the softness of a brush's bristles. As she turned to look at poplar canvas frames, she suddenly glimpsed a figure moving through the crowd just beyond the booth's cloth walls. A flash of darkness amid the lightness of the market. She gasped, sure she was imagining things, that her thoughts had summoned him.

Surely her Hades was not here in the market, not now.

She hardly dared to breathe as she tiptoed to the edge of the booth. The glimpse was gone. If he had been there at all, he was swallowed up by the crowds now. Yet she still felt so strange, as if a warmth danced over her skin and the light of the day around her was grown even more vivid.

She went up on tiptoe, her gaze quickly scanning the walkways. She knew she should not be looking. Even if he *was* there, she should hide in the booth until he was gone. She didn't know him. Florentine ladies were not meant to converse with strange men. She couldn't be distracted now, not from her art or her family.

Yet she felt a cold, sinking disappointment that he was gone so fast. If he had ever been there at all and was not just her fanciful imagination.

'*Signora*, how may I assist you today?' a voice suddenly said behind her.

Startled, Isabella spun around to find the

proprietor watching her. He was a short, rotund, balding man in a russet doublet and apron stained with ochre, a figure who should surely be jolly and laughing. Yet he watched her warily and Isabella was again reminded she was a stranger there.

'*Signora?*' he asked again. 'Are you sent on an errand for someone?'

'I…' Isabella began.

'The lady is surely on an errand for herself, Signor Rastrelli,' someone else said, in a deep, velvet-smooth voice lightly touched with a hint of some secret amusement. A voice she had thought of far too often after last night.

'For she is an artist herself, a friend of Signor Botticelli and kinswoman to Caterina Strozzi,' the voice went on.

Isabella glanced back over her shoulder to see that it *was* her Hades. He had disappeared from the crowd only to suddenly reappear before her, as if he was lord of the Underworld in truth.

Her heart pounded a little faster to see his eyes watching her, such a clear, pale sea-green colour that seemed to see so much more than she wanted to reveal. She smiled tentatively, but was glad she didn't yet need to speak. Her throat felt too tight.

'*Signora?*' the merchant said, his wariness fading into hope for a new customer. 'You are a student of the great Botticelli?'

Isabella glanced up at Hades from under her lashes. He gave her an encouraging smile. 'Nay, not a student. Merely an amateur who enjoys sketching. But I do require some supplies.'

'Some scarlet pigment, perhaps, *signora*?' the merchant said, all eagerness now. 'Or mayhap lapis, for a Madonna's robe? I just had a delivery this morning. The very best.'

'Oh,' Isabella whispered as he held out a tiny box that held a block of that most precious of brilliant blues. She dared not even touch it. Somehow she could feel Hades watching her and it made her cheeks burn too warm. She wanted to turn away, to hide her face from him so he couldn't read her thoughts.

But she wouldn't give him the amusement

of making her feel like a silly country maiden. She carefully folded her hands at her waist and held her head high.

'Just some charcoal sticks today, *signor*,' she said. 'And mayhap those two brushes here. I will order more later when I know my requirements.'

As the merchant wrapped up her purchases, Isabella wandered away among the other wares. She couldn't lose herself in them as she had before, for she was all too aware of the man behind her.

'You will study with Botticelli while you are here?' he asked.

Isabella shook her head. 'I shall be far too busy with my cousin to spend much time painting.'

'Caterina Strozzi?' he said. There was a strange taut thread to his tone.

She glanced back at him, startled, and he looked back at her with his handsome, chiselled face completely expressionless. 'You know her?'

He gave her a quick smile and any tension was dissipated. 'Everyone in Florence knows of the beautiful Caterina. I am surprised she can bear to have her sun eclipsed by such a lovely cousin. If she was wise, she would have kept you far away.'

Isabella laughed at his blatant flattery. 'I do have a looking glass, *signor*, so I can detect falseness in such pretty words. You must read your Petrarch and find more convincing language.'

He laughed too, ruefully. He shook his head and the sunlight glinted on his glossy dark hair. 'I am no poet, true. I can only speak as I see. Your cousin is truly a famous Florentine beauty, but beauty such as hers soon fades away.' He reached out and gently, softly, stroked one fingertip along a strand of loose hair that had worked its way free of her netted caul. 'The beauty of the night only increases as it conceals.'

Isabella shivered under his touch. She wanted to arch under it, like a cat, but she slid away.

She wanted to see what he would do next, this most unpredictable man.

And she wanted to believe his words, far more than she should.

The merchant came back with her purchases, giving her a welcome distraction. But Hades stayed with her as she left the booth and she was fully conscious of him there by her side.

The market was not as crowded now, the stalls' wares diminished as the sun blazed higher in the sky. Caterina's pageboy was nowhere to be seen.

And Isabella feared she was quite turned around. She couldn't remember which way she should go.

He seemed to sense her uncertainty. 'Shall I escort you home, *signorina*? The streets of Florence can be most baffling for those who don't know it, remember.'

Isabella laughed. Yes, she did want him to go with her, though at the same time she wanted to be free of the confusion that came over her when he was near. 'You will save me again?

They are baffling, yes, and can be frightening. But also most beautiful, I think.' She shielded her eyes from the warm golden light and studied the red, sloping tiles of the tall roofs against the soft white of the walls and the bright blue of the sky. Brunelleschi's dome could be glimpsed in the distance, an elaborate pattern of dark red and mellow yellow. 'Have you lived here long, then, *signor*, to know these streets?'

He frowned. 'Long, aye. I know it well. My true home is in the hills, at my family's villa, but I will happily be your guide to more beauties of Florence today, if you will let me.'

Isabella laughed. She knew very well she shouldn't follow such a rogue anywhere. Country maid she might be; fool she hoped she was not. She had just arrived in the city and was far from finding her footing there. She felt dizzy, almost drunk with the beauty and activity of the city, with all the colours and scents and noises. And, yes, dizzy with the intriguing mysteries she saw in this man's eyes. She couldn't let herself be swept away by it.

But surely just one little, short walk couldn't hurt? It was such a beautiful day and this man intrigued her so very much.

'I can walk with you now, if you are quite sure, *signor*,' she said with a laugh. 'Yet I must demand one thing first.'

He tilted back his head to study her, a small frown touching the edges of his beautiful mouth. 'A demand, *signorina*?'

His wariness made her laugh even more. Surely ladies had demanded much of him. She was surprised he wasn't constantly followed by an army of them.

'I must ask your name, *signor*,' she said. 'I cannot go on calling you…' She bit her lip to hold inside that last word before it was too late. Before he could see her ridiculous fantasies.

His brow arched. 'What *do* you call me, then?'

Isabella shook her head. She couldn't tell him she thought of him as Hades, the darkly brooding god of the Underworld. It might make him think she wanted to play his Persephone and be carried off by him to his shadowy kingdom.

She felt her cheeks turn warm and drew the fluttering edge of the sheer veil on her cap closer around her face. 'I am an artist of sorts, *signor*. I confess that when I meet new people, I begin to envision them as characters in paintings. That's all. It's silly.'

He laughed and his handsome face glowed. She longed to hear him laugh more. 'I am intrigued,' he said. More customers crowded into the small booth and he gently laid his hand at the small of her back to escort her into the sunlit jostle of the market. Though the touch was light as a butterfly's wing and just as fleeting, she could feel the heat of it through the wool and linen of her gown.

It made her shiver.

'What would you paint me as, then?' he said. He stayed close to her as they made their way through the crowd. The sun had climbed higher in the sky, warm and amber-gold.

Isabella shrugged. Indeed, a painting *had* begun to form in her mind, a work of shadows and flames, a jewelled Underworld throne, a proffered pomegranate of temptation held out to a pale maiden. An elaborate scene beyond her skill level. But if she could keep visiting Botticelli's studio, watch how he worked…

And not be distracted by a man like the one who stood with her now. That would be difficult.

'Perhaps a court jester,' she said lightly, dodging around two small boys chasing a stray cat. 'I do hear the Medici and the Pazzi like to keep such around their *palazzi*, to juggle and cavort around their banquet tables. If I were to paint a supper party…' She shrugged.

He laughed again and she felt strangely proud to have invoked his mirth. She had a feeling it was quite rare. 'Is that what you think of me? That I am a jester?'

Isabella shielded her eyes from the sun, and pretended to carefully study his face, though in truth she already knew it in too much detail. The sharp angles of his cheekbone and jaw, the straight nose, as if it was carved from marble. The tumble of his dark hair over his brow. 'I cannot know what to think, *signor*, when I do not even know your true name.'

His laughter faded, but a smile remained. 'I am called Orlando.'

Only Orlando? She was sure he must bear some grand surname. His clothes, though dark in colour, were of the finest materials and perfectly cut, and he walked with a confidence that could only be born of careful breeding. But just Orlando was all she needed now. She was enjoying their imaginary game of 'who are you' too much to let it go just yet.

'And I am Isabella,' she said, making a small curtsy. 'What shall you show me of this fair city first, Orlando?'

'Santa Maria del Fiore, of course! Come with me.'

Isabella laughed as he took her hand and drew her with him out of the market. He seemed as charmingly eager as a boy to show her his city and she found herself caught up in his enthusiasm. They left the bustle and crowds of the *mercato* behind, turning on to quieter lanes, narrow and winding. Orlando offered her his arm and she took it, drawing her veil closer in case anyone saw them.

But no one paid them any attention, everyone was too busy hurrying on their own errands. Orlando led her through the city and she loved seeing it through his eyes. The sounds and smells, the colours, were all so very vivid, so alive, and she longed to capture it all in paint.

To either side of them on the winding lanes rose the palaces of the great families. Like her cousins' house, they presented thick, blank, fortress-like walls to the world, hiding treasures inside. Grille-screened balconies overhung the walkways, and occasionally Isabella glimpsed a pale face peering out, a flutter of bright silks.

But above all she was aware of the man at her side. The tense, lean strength of his arm under her hand, the heat of his body. The deep sound of his voice as he pointed out landmarks to her. The way he leaned close to speak to her; the clean, crisp, lemony scent of his cologne. She never wanted this walk, this perfect day, to end.

They passed the Medici *palazzo*, the largest house in the city, and Isabella heard the toll of the church bells growing louder. Orlando guided her on to the Via de Martelli and the great cathedral rose before them, its famous rose-red dome soaring to the sky.

Isabella went still, awestruck by its beauty. The elaborately patterned marble walls and carved doors, giving way to the stark, impossible simplicity of the dome.

She sensed Orlando smiling down at her and she pinched her lips together to keep from gaping like a simple country girl.

Orlando laughed. 'It is astonishing, is it not? That such beauty could be right here before us.'

Isabella could only nod. 'I have seen sketches of it before, but could hardly warrant it was real.'

'Come, you must see inside.'

Isabella followed him through the doors and for a moment the darkness after the bright light of day blinded her. She blinked and saw it was not so dark after all. Light flickered from hundreds of candles and filtered down from dozens of stained-glass windows. Patterns of jewel-like greens, reds, blues and violets fell across the mosaic patterns of the stone floor, making them shimmer as if they were alive.

She shivered as the cool air swept along the arches. Orlando drew her closer to his side and they drifted along the length of the nave.

Isabella studied the images of the saints who peered down at them from the walls. She wondered what they thought about all they saw, all they heard. The space was so tall, so vast, that it seemed almost empty, yet in reality crowds of people drifted past.

At last they reached the end of the nave and the space opened up into the soaring light-filled space of the dome. It was like nothing she had ever seen, as if at any moment they would be raised up into heaven itself. And Orlando had given it to her.

'Would you like to see a secret space?' he whispered to her, a hint of laughter in his voice.

She laughed and looked up into his eyes.

They seemed to smile down at her, at odds with his Underworld demeanour. What a fascinating puzzle he was. 'Could there be anything better than this?'

'Come with me.' He took her hand and led her past the high altar, where several ladies knelt in prayer, their satin skirts spread around them. Mystified, intrigued, Isabella followed him to a twisting, narrow flight of stairs. They hurried up it, their footsteps muffled, and she found herself high above the crowd in an empty choir loft.

Isabella leaned on the gilded railing and stared down at the crowds swirling along the aisles, vanishing in and out of the shadows of the different family chapels. From so high, their voices were mere whispers. Like the rush of the waters of the Arno beneath the bridges. Here, the rest of the world was far away and she was closed in by the hush and surrounded by the otherworldly beauty of the frescoes over her head.

Yet she wasn't alone. Orlando stood beside

her, so close his velvet sleeve almost brushed hers as he braced his hands on the railing. She was achingly aware of his nearness, of the warmth of his body, the spicy scent of him.

He was like no one else she'd ever known. He was so charming as he led her through the city, showing her all its glories as if they belonged only to him. He had made her laugh and forget about how very new and strange life was now. How far away her home was.

But here, in the incense-wreathed hush of the church, she remembered why she first thought of him as a dark lord. He stared down at the bright world below, so solemn and watchful, his thoughts seeming so far away. His lean, strong body was still, tense, as if he waited for the smallest sign of danger to attack. Like a sleek black panther she had seen once at a market, rippling, prowling, all caged danger.

It made her shiver again.

He glanced down at her and for an instant he looked surprised, as if he had forgotten she was there. Then he smiled, a brilliant, blinding grin, and leaned even closer to her.

'Well, Isabella?' he said lightly. 'What do you think of Florence's jewel?'

'I think it is surpassing beautiful, of course,' she answered slowly. 'The paintings, the glass, the marble—nothing could be more grand. Yet I think the fields and trees of my father's land are just as lovely.'

'I see something before me even more lovely than anything I could imagine,' he said roughly.

Isabella stared up at him, caught by his extraordinary eyes. She swayed towards him and his arms came around her, holding her close. Suddenly it felt as if there was only the two of them in the world. Suddenly she felt completely safe.

She slid her arms around his waist and closed her eyes. He pressed a gentle kiss to her brow and she smiled. He laughed softly and his lips touched her temple, her cheek, leaving a ribbon of fire wherever his lips brushed her skin.

She shivered with the desire that swept through her, making her very toes tingle.

At last, at last, his lips touched hers. Once, twice, and again, deeper, harder. He groaned against her mouth and the kiss caught flame.

He dragged her even closer to his hard, tall body and they fit together perfectly, as if meant to be just like that. Just together.

Isabella went up on her toes, her mouth opening beneath his. She had only been kissed a few times before, country lads, and it felt nothing at all like *this*. So wondrous and overwhelming. His tongue, light and skilful, touched the tip of hers enticingly before sweeping deeper.

She twined her arms around his neck, holding him tightly as if that dream could vanish. But he seemed to have no intention of leaving her. He pulled her up to him and the kiss turned desperate, heated and blurry, full of a need she didn't even know was in her. Her whole body felt heavy and hot, narrowed to only that perfect touch of his lips.

A burst of sound echoing from the sanctuary below was the only thing that shattered the spell of the kiss. Isabella fell backwards and tried to catch her breath as she stared up at him. He smiled at her, but he also seemed to have a hard time breathing. His eyes were dark as a winter forest.

'I…I should go,' she whispered. She glanced at the large clock above the cathedral doors and saw that the hour did indeed grow late. But if she had her wish, she would never leave this choir loft.

He nodded. 'Let me see you towards your home,' he said and held out his hand to her. His voice sounded roughened and she was glad he seemed affected by their kiss, too. She wouldn't want to be alone in this—whatever it was.

Isabella took Orlando's hand as he led her down the last of the steep stone steps. He lifted her off her feet on the last rise, spinning her in a half circle as she laughed giddily. The whole day felt like a glorious dream!

'You should always laugh like that, fairest Isabella,' he said. He stared down into her eyes, slowly sliding her to her feet. 'There is little such perfect music in this city.'

'Indeed?' she said. She had to hold tight to his lean shoulders to keep from falling. 'But Florence seems merry. My cousin says there are dances and banquets all the time.'

He drew her closer for an instant—a moment that seemed to last for an eternity. As she looked up into his startling sea-green eyes, she felt as if she had fallen deep into a warm summer pool. It pulled her down and down, until she couldn't break free. She wasn't even sure if she *wanted* to be free.

In those eyes, in that one unguarded instant, she read so many things. Sadness, hope, disbelief. All the things she felt herself.

'Don't be fooled by masks, Isabella,' he whispered close to her ear. His warm breath brushed softly against her skin, making her tremble. 'You are an artist. Surely you know better than most what lies beneath such glitter. Silks and velvets are a thin concealment.'

His long, elegant hands tightened on her

arms, drawing her up on her toes. She braced her palms on his chest and felt the warm, quick rhythm of his heartbeat under the velvet and leather of his doublet.

Images flashed through her mind, like bursts of sun showers. Caterina's pale, beautiful face against the shimmering tapestries of her chamber. Giuliano de Medici and his handsome friends jostling together. Botticelli's painting, all elegance and grace and light. Matteo's hearty laughter. The soaring dome high over her head, soaring to heaven. Orlando's lips against hers. Which of them were false? What should she trust, what should she beware of?

She suddenly felt overwhelmed, as if the summer pool had turned icy and was dragging her down. She swayed dizzily.

A burst of giggles somewhere in the sanctuary, echoing off the marble, brought her to her senses. She wasn't trapped in some dizzying dream, she was in the real, sunlit world. She could burst free at any moment.

She only feared she did not quite want to be free.

She stepped back, letting his hands fall away from her. She laughed and spun around, letting the shadows and light of the vast church wash over her.

'What riddles!' she said. 'Does everyone here speak thus? It's a miracle that conversations don't last for days and days.'

'Isabella…' Orlando began, his tone tense.

'Isabella! Is that you?' another voice rang out, loud and hearty, full of laughter. Her cousin Matteo's voice.

She whirled around again to see Matteo striding towards her, his gold-and-violet striped cloak swirling around him. He waved to her. When she turned back around, Orlando was nowhere to be seen.

Bewildered, Isabella scanned the crowds around her. She saw friends of Caterina's from Botticelli's studio, women in scarlet and black and silver, men in plumed caps, priests in their dark hassocks. But no Orlando. He had vanished as if he'd never been there at all.

A strange, cold loneliness swept over her. She shook it away as her cousin came closer, but still she couldn't help but long for Orlando again.

Matteo took her hands in his and drew her close to kiss her cheeks. He smelled different from Orlando, richer, more flowery, tinged with wine. His friends tumbled behind him like a pack of the jesters Isabella had teased Orlando about.

'Are you feeling pious today, cousin?' Matteo said teasingly.

'I was told I should see the beauties of Florence,' she answered, struggling to make herself feel normal, to be in the present moment. 'Is the dome not the greatest beauty of all?'

A frown shadowed his golden face. 'You shouldn't be wandering the city alone, cousin,' he said warningly. 'It is often unsafe.'

'I...' Isabella glanced over her shoulder, only

to find Orlando had indeed melted away. Had she dreamed the whole day?

'I had one of Caterina's pages with me, but he wanted to play dice in the marketplace while I prayed,' she said with a laugh. 'I saw no harm in it. This is a church, is it not?'

'He will lose his position, then,' Matteo said.

'Surely going to church cannot be all that perilous?' Isabella said. Perilous only to her feelings, perhaps. For those moments with Orlando had her head spinning. He was what she had feared for so long—wanting to be with someone too much. And now he was gone.

Matteo's gaze scanned the marble walls and gilded monuments like a hunter waiting for a boar, his eyes narrowed. Isabella tried to see what he saw, but she did not have a Florentine vision. She saw only three ladies in dark purple and deep crimson satin, their golden hair wreathed with the fluttering, sheer silk of their veils as they giggled together. A cardinal in his red damask robes, as dignified as a ship in sail while petitioners scurried behind him. A cluster of men in the blue-and-gold livery of the Pazzi family, laughing raucously.

'You never know what may lurk nearby, my fair cousin,' Matteo said. 'This can be a jealous city and we are a favoured family, friends with the Medici. It is best to be always wary. Come, I will escort you home. Surely Caterina will be looking for you.'

Isabella accepted her cousin's offered arm. Yet even as she smiled at his pleasantries, she couldn't help but cast one more glance back at the shadows of the church. Her Hades was not there at all.

Matteo Strozzi.

Orlando watched through the twists and turns of the crowd as Isabella took Strozzi's arm and walked with him out of the church. His bravo friends tumbled after them, giving Orlando only a glimpse of her dark-blue cloak, the simple twisted braids of her black hair under her sheer veil. Strozzi bent his head to say something to her, making her smile. *Damn him.*

Only the knowledge that Isabella was his kinswoman, and that Strozzi was unlikely to hurt her because of his own family honour, held Orlando back from chasing them down and snatching Isabella away from him. But one day he would no longer be able to hold himself back.

At the end of the wide marble aisle, she paused and glanced over her shoulder. Orlando knew she was too far away to see him, but he stepped back into the shadows anyway, watching her carefully. It would do no good for Strozzi to see him now, not in front of her. Sweet, lovely Isabella. How could she be related to the Strozzi at all?

She seemed disappointed by whatever she found. She drew her cloak hood over her hair and vanished into the flood of sunlight beyond the sacred shadows of the church.

Maledizione. He could barely hold himself back from running after her.

Orlando rubbed his hand hard over his jaw, cursing himself for a fool. Lucretia had told him he was a questing knight, that one day he would find the jewel he sought without even knowing it and he would be lost. He had only laughed at her, called her a romantic. But when he looked into the darkness of Isabella's eyes, it felt like a sudden flash of just such a thing. Of finding a rare treasure he hadn't even known he sought, that he had scoffed to think even existed.

It was startling, enough to almost bring him to his knees. Like a flash of lightning through his body.

But he did not feel like a questing, gallant knight in some poem. He felt as if he was the court jester Isabella had teased him about, a fool to fate.

He'd lost his innocence in the taverns of Florence so long ago and the last of his shining, tattered shreds of hope when Maria Lorenza was injured. Matteo Strozzi had seen to that. And now, when he at last felt a glimmer of such rare wonder again, Strozzi was there to snatch it away.

When he looked at Isabella, he saw a goddess.

A saint, wide-eyed with wonder at life. Yet she was kin to Strozzi and lost to him already. That hope was like the glitter of a star, beautiful, entrancing, but impossible to ever touch.

For he had vowed one day to take his final revenge on Strozzi. And he would wound Isabella in the fulfilment of that promise. One more innocent destroyed by life in Florence.

'Orlando,' a woman's voice called, low and musical.

He glanced over his shoulder to find Lucretia gliding towards him. A sheer purple-silk veil fluttered over her golden hair. The elaborate curls and waves glittered with ropes of pearls and amethysts, sparkling, but her face was solemn.

'Praying for your soul, are you?' she said with a sad little smile. She held out her hand for him to kiss.

Orlando tried to smile at her, to show her only the careless face he showed all the world. But she would not be fooled. 'You know my soul is too blackened for mere prayers. It would take all my fortune to buy enough Masses.'

Lucretia shook her head. She tucked her bejewelled hand into the crook of his arm and led him out of the shadows. They paused before the Annunciation in the altarpiece. The Madonna's face, a pale, serene oval, somehow made him think of Isabella and the wonder in her eyes when she looked around the cathedral.

'Shadowed it certainly is, but never as black as you declare. You looked so very sad just then. What has happened?'

Orlando studied the face of the painted Madonna high above them. She did look like Isabella, with that bright curiosity about the world around her in her eyes. The innocence.

'Do you remember, Lucretia, when you told me I would one day find what I sought? The one thing I am meant to do in the world?' he said.

He could feel her watching him. 'I do. I have long thought that. Have you found it?'

He shook his head. 'My purpose was set long

ago, come what may. And I have not such faith in myself that I have only been seeking a good purpose to give my life meaning. I have only sought pleasure. And I have always been lucky enough to find it.'

'But something *has* happened. Something has changed. I see it in your eyes.'

Orlando was silent for a long moment, still studying the painted Madonna. He saw Isabella's smile again, the sudden rare gift of her laughter. 'You know of everyone in Florence, Lucretia. Have you heard of a woman named Isabella, kinswoman to Matteo and Caterina Strozzi?'

Lucretia tilted her head to one side as she searched her copious memory. 'Isabella Strozzi?'

'I do not know. She knows Signor Botticelli.'

'I have not heard of any new arrivals named Isabella. Is she young, marriageable?'

'Young, but not of the first youth.' Wiser and richer than that, but still innocent of the world. Perfect. 'Artistic.'

'And pretty, I would wager.' Lucretia laughed.

'I am most intrigued, Orlando. It has been a very long time since you showed such interest in a respectable lady. Never, I would say.'

'I cannot be interested in her,' he answered.

'Nevertheless, I have been in search of a project and you have given me one. I will find out what I can about this mysterious Isabella. But what shall you do with this information?'

Orlando thought again of Isabella's smile—and the way she took her cousin's arm. Her cousin, Orlando's sworn enemy. 'I do not know what I will do,' he said truthfully. 'Yet somehow—I need to know more.'

Lucretia smiled. 'You can do nothing more today, Orlando. Come with me to my *palazzo*. Many of your old friends are coming later for supper. We always have an amusing time. I think you need a distraction from the mysterious lady for an afternoon. I've never seen you quite like this.'

Lucretia was right. He did need a distraction. Isabella was kin to the Strozzi, after all; surely she could not be all that she appeared.

'Very well, fairest Lucretia,' he said, raising her perfumed hand for a quick, teasing kiss. 'Distracted I shall be.'

She laughed. 'Somehow, I do not believe that.'

Chapter Six

Isabella made her way slowly through the market, half-afraid she should turn and dash back to Caterina's *palazzo* before she was missed. Before she made even more of a fool of herself. She found her hands were trembling as she drew the hood of her cloak closer.

Yet something in her wouldn't let her turn back, something powerful and strong. As magically inexplicable as the dome over the cathedral. She didn't know where to begin looking. Surely he didn't even want to be found. Yet here she was, searching none the less.

It was very early. The sun, creeping higher in the lapis-blue sky, was still a burnt pink at the edges. The merchants were just setting up their wares, laughing and calling out sleepily to each other as they laid out piles of glistening fish, pyramids of jewel-like fruit, bolts of ribbons. She couldn't quite remember where the art supplier was, yet still she looked.

Isabella turned a corner in a narrow alleyway and suddenly that miraculous dome soared up into view. The new light of day turned it to a mellow rosy-red, sparkling on the pure white marble beneath. She remembered standing beneath that glorious space with Orlando, his arms coming around her, his mouth covering hers in that soul-stealing kiss. A kiss she had lain awake remembering all night.

She suddenly swayed, a wave of dizziness breaking over her at the memory, and reached out to lean against the stone wall. Images flashed through her mind like hastily glimpsed paintings, the gilded mosaics in the church, the whirl of people, the hush of the balcony where there was only Orlando and herself, wrapped up in each other.

That kiss had been like nothing else she had

ever known, or could even imagine. The very ground beneath her feet had swollen like the wave of a flooding river and burst, drowning her, and nothing could surely be the same again. It was as if she glimpsed the emotions only evoked by paint or charcoal on canvas.

Yet then he had vanished, just as he had that day he saved her from the thieves. Disappeared as if he was one of her dreams, half-hidden, desperately sought, but always elusive.

She closed her eyes for an instant and in that darkness she saw again the way he looked at her after they kissed. The sadness and longing, the burning fire of passion, that made her want nothing more than to leap into those flames and be completely consumed.

She knew she couldn't have been fooled by that glow in his otherworldly eyes. There was no artifice there in that instant, only raw, burning life.

Yet there was that fathomless darkness, too. That darkness that had frightened her the first time she met him and she saw the depths of anger he held deep inside of himself. That was there as well, fighting with the light of desire.

She opened her eyes and saw that the sun had risen even higher in the sky, setting the dawn afire. That darkness in Orlando drew her just as the light of his laughter did. She was much too intrigued with him. She *had* to know more and that was what drew her out so secretly to the market again that morning.

She whirled around and rushed out of the alleyway, plunging back into the noise and colour of the marketplace. It was more crowded now, customers clamouring to buy the freshest wares, shrieking and laughing with their friends, arguing with the merchants over their prices. Isabella scanned each covered booth until she finally found the art supplier.

'Ah, *signora* the artist!' he cried when she ducked into the booth. 'You have returned. For some of my very fine lapis, mayhap?'

Isabella laughed. The familiar, comforting scents of the crushed pigments and liquid washes wrapping around her helped to steady her, to remind her of her mission in the market that day. She had to find Orlando. No matter how very much her mind told her she should not see him again, her heart and all her artistic senses pushed her to find him. To figure out what hold he had over her.

And her heart had been too long ignored in her safe, quiet country life. It wouldn't be silent now.

'Later, perhaps, when my skills improve,' she answered. 'At the moment, I require some information you might have, *signor*. About the man I met here yesterday, the tall one in black.'

The man frowned and shook his head doubtfully, his gaze shifting away. 'I am not very certain…'

Five minutes and a small handful of coins later, and Isabella had the information she needed. She asked directions of a fishmonger and turned towards a quarter of the city nearer the river, where the art supply merchant said Orlando had lodgings.

As she made her way through the swelling crowds, growing even thicker as the morning slid towards noon, she realized how very little she actually knew about Orlando. What was his family? What did he do with his days? He knew of art and philosophy, and he seemed to see into *her* heart all too well. Yet what was in his? What was the solemnity, the secrecy, she glimpsed in his eyes?

She was half-afraid to find out, but she had to. Something had pulled her towards him ever since he saved her that first day she arrived and it drew her still, like a gilded rope between them.

The neighbourhood the merchant directed her to was not as grand as Caterina's square of glittering *palazzi*. But neither did it hold the air of cracked neglect like the deserted square where she nearly came to grief before Orlando appeared like an avenging angel. It was bustling, crowded, prosperous, with an air of energy and purpose. Bright boxes of spring flowers gleamed outside open windows, while laundry snapped in the breeze and children ran past, laughing.

Surely anyone who lodged in such a street could not hide anything *too* sinister, Isabella thought as she looked around her. It seemed so—ordinary, so everyday, next to Orlando's mystery and beauty.

She found the house where he was said to have his lodgings, yet she found she didn't have to summon up the courage to knock on the door after all. She glimpsed a tall figure in black through the crowd, appearing and disappearing between the hurrying figures. She almost called out to him in a sudden surge of joy at seeing him, but something held her back. She cautiously made her way closer and was glad she didn't follow her first impulse. It seemed Orlando was not alone.

A lady held on to his arm, laughing up at him as he smiled at something she said. It was not merely any woman, but quite the most beautiful woman Isabella had ever seen. Her golden hair was twisted atop her head in elaborate, jewel-twined braids, barely concealed by the sheer lavender silk of her veil. Her face was a pale, perfect oval set off by arched blonde brows and the shimmer of amethyst earrings. She held on to Orlando's arm easily, casually, as if she knew him very well.

And he smiled at her, one of those perfect sun-flash smiles that were so rare.

Isabella's burst of elation seemed to collapse in on itself and she shivered. Yes, Orlando had kissed her, talked to her, intrigued her, yet truly she did not know him.

She felt like a fool for trying to seek him out.

She started to turn away, to lose herself once again in the crowd, but the beautiful woman suddenly turned her head and saw Isabella there. Her eyes widened, as if she somehow recognized Isabella, and she tugged at Orlando's arm so that he turned as well.

There was no running away now.

His smile wavered, vanished, but then it returned full force. Isabella went up on her toes, as if her body would run to him even against her own will, and she had to force herself to stay where she was. To not look away from him and thus reveal all the foolish hopes that drove her that day.

He murmured something to the woman, who nodded. She gave Isabella one last quizzical glance and disappeared into the crowd. Orlando hurried towards Isabella and she was glad she hadn't run away after all. His smile was worth staying to see.

'This is a fine sight for me this morning, Signorina Isabella,' he said lightly. 'Are you in search of art supplies again?'

'I—think perhaps I took a wrong turn somewhere,' Isabella murmured, dazzled as she looked up at him. There was no darkness in him at that moment, no hint of anger. Just that alluring smile, a bright light in his eyes that drew her in all over again. 'I should not take you away from your companion...'

Orlando glanced over his shoulder and Isabella saw that the golden woman had vanished.

'Lucretia is an old friend. I think we are well met today, you and I.'

A friend only? Isabella wanted to believe that, wanted to believe he was as happy to see her as she was him. His smile seemed to speak the truth of that. 'Are we indeed?'

'Aye. I thought much last night about our time in the church,' he said, his smile flickering into solemnity. 'I should not have left you as I did. It was most ungallant.'

Isabella remembered how puzzled she had been, how she had wondered about him. Yet seeing him again seemed to erase all doubts. 'I had met with my cousin. I was surely in no danger again.'

'But we were not able to finish our tour of Florence's beautiful sites,' he said with a flash of a smile, a roguish one now that made her laugh.

How very changeable he was, she thought. From darkness to sunny light in an instant. It made her feel quite dizzy. 'Where would you recommend I look next, then?'

'If you have time, perhaps a walk by the river? Then I will see you safely home. You remember how unpredictable the city can be.'

Isabella nodded. The thieves he had saved her from that first day had indeed been fearsome, but she was now quite sure the greatest danger in Florence was *him*. At least for her. His kiss had made her forget, yet now she remembered the blonde woman who smiled at him. He was a part of this city, this world, and she was not.

But still—still she wanted to look at his smile just a little longer. 'Very well,' she said. 'A walk sounds perfect on such a lovely day.'

His smile flashed again. 'Come, then, let me show you.'

He offered his arm and Isabella laid her hand lightly on his velvet sleeve. She could feel the strength and heat of him under her touch and it made her smile.

Orlando told her of the sites they passed, the churches and fine *palazzi*, until they reached the river itself. They strolled out on to an arched stone bridge and found a quieter, more private niche that looked down at the water. The noise and clamour of the city faded away there.

Isabella leaned over the stone edge of the bridge to gaze down at the water. The fresh, pale golden sunlight sparkled on the rippling waves, dappling the boats that passed beneath. It all looked so enchanted, bathed in rosy-gold light, yet still dark at the edges. Just like Orlando.

'Have you always lived here?' she asked. She glanced over at Orlando just in time to see a shadow flicker over his handsome face. But it was gone quickly, hidden by that smile.

'My father's estate was near Umbria,' he said, perfectly calm, perfectly impersonal.

'Was?' she asked, curious.

'It is still there, but I seldom return to it. I had a sister, you see, who was very dear to me. She died there, and I—do not like to be reminded of her and what happened to her,' he said, still so horribly quiet. 'The distractions of the city suit me better now.'

Isabella studied the houses and church spires

before her, so golden, so beautiful, so perfectly suited to hiding all secrets. It did seem the perfect place to escape grief and sorrow. Her heart ached that the sorrow was his. 'I can see that. I also wanted to escape my home, to see more of the wide world. But I miss my father's house, I miss knowing I belong there, what will happen next. Here, I never know at all.'

'There are too many memories at my father's house now,' Orlando said softly. He looked away from the vista before him and suddenly smiled again. 'Here, everything is like new with every fresh day. I never know what I will see or who I will meet. It is an adventure.'

Isabella laughed ruefully. 'Like a lost country mouse in need of rescue?'

Orlando did not laugh. He reached out and gently, softly, smoothed back a lock of her hair that had fallen from its pins. The tips of his fingers brushed over her skin and she shivered.

'Like beautiful artists, who make me see the world in a whole new light,' he whispered.

Flustered, warm with blushes, Isabella looked

away. 'I think that is what brought me to Florence. To see the world in a new way,' she said. 'I want to create art, to see made manifest on a canvas my vision of the world. All the beauty and the fear, too. The transcendence that always seems just beyond reach.'

That was what *he* was. All transcendent beauty, light and darkness all together. Just like what she saw when she was lost in a painting, falling deep into a whirlpool of aching emotions she could never understand in real life. The realization of it, of him, made her want to cry. She closed her eyes and tried to force the aching tears away.

Suddenly, she felt the soft brush of his hand against her cheek again. His touch was feather light, yet it seemed to leave shimmering sparks across her skin. She jumped, startled, and his palm cupped her cheek to hold her with him as if she was made of the most fragile, precious porcelain.

His touch slid slowly, carefully, down the side of her neck beneath her cloak hood, dislodging it from her hair. His fingertips toyed with the ribbon tie of her sleeve. She felt the heat of his hand through the wool and muslin, and thought again of how he was a god, a Hades, sent to tempt mortals. And he was so good at it.

His other hand came to the back of her head and he drew her even closer. She felt his breath whisper over her skin.

'So beautiful,' he whispered. There was no hint of teasing laughter in his voice. The words seemed torn from him, aching. He stared down at her intently, his eyes darkened, and she couldn't turn away.

She felt suddenly far too vulnerable, as if he was looking again into her deepest heart. But he held her still, his fingers twined in her hair. He didn't hurt her, yet neither would he let her go.

'Not as beautiful as you,' she said hoarsely.

He shook his head, still staring down at her as if he would memorize her. He bent his head and kissed the small, soft, sensitive spot just below her ear. She felt the shocking touch of the tip of his tongue on her skin, the light scrape of his teeth, and it made her tremble with the force of the emotion that rolled through her.

She gasped and clutched at the front of his fine velvet doublet as she tried to keep from falling. Her eyes closed as she fell deep into the hot, swirling waters of sensation. It was just as when he had kissed her before and she knew now it was not merely kissing that made her feel thus—it was only him. He made something so deep and instinctive rise up in her, until she knew only him. The rest of the world didn't exist.

His arms closed hard around her waist and he lifted her against him to catch her mouth with his. He tasted of wine and that rich darkness that was only him, that she craved far too much. She wrapped her hands around the back of his neck and held on to him tightly. The rough silk of his dark hair curled over her fingers.

She heard him moan deep inside his throat as his tongue slid over hers and she met him eagerly. He was so wondrous, so very warm and alive, and he made her feel as if she was waking up to the real world at last.

He made her feel *too* much. Too hot, too cold, too scared, too excited. The force of her feelings frightened her, as if the pool that had been so warm, so enticing only a moment before, was drowning her and soon she would vanish into him.

Orlando seemed to sense her sudden rush of fear. His lips tore away from hers and he pressed his forehead against hers. He went very still as their ragged, mingled breath slowed.

Isabella was suddenly aware of the world around them, the laughter of people outside their hidden spot, the rush of the river, the wheeling birds overhead.

'I—I must go,' she whispered. She turned away from the piercing, pale light of his eyes and pulled her hood up around her again. If only she could hide her heart so easily. 'My cousin will be looking for me.'

'Let me see you home,' he said, his voice slightly rough.

Isabella remembered how he had disappeared in the cathedral and her confusion increased. What was he about with her? Did he feel as she did? Or was she merely being that country mouse again, unsure of the ways of Florence? 'I should go alone,' she said.

'Then I will watch you until you are safely there,' he said firmly, as if she would not be allowed to argue that point. 'No one will see me at your cousin's home.'

Isabella just wanted to get home, to be quiet and think. She nodded and turned to make her way out of their hidden hollow of the bridge into the crowd again. People pressed close on all sides, drawing her back into the real world.

At the foot of the bridge, she glanced back. True to his word, he was nowhere to be seen, yet she would vow she could feel him watching her. Her dark angel.

At last she reached Caterina's *palazzo*. The

footman opened the door for her, and as soon as she was closed in alone in the cool marble hush of the hall, she collapsed back against the wall.

She felt a smile tug at her lips, entirely against her will, but it would not be denied. And it was only from *him*. It was only Orlando who made her so giddy. She lifted the hem of her skirts and ran as fast as she could up the stairs.

Orlando couldn't help but laugh as he watched Isabella glance over her shoulder at the door of the *palazzo*, an anxious look on her face. He knew very well she couldn't see him, but he revelled in that one last glimpse of her.

Isabella was like no one else he had ever known. There was a light inside of her, a force of life he had rarely glimpsed in anyone else, and that light beckoned him closer and closer. If he came too near, he knew he would fall into her heat and forget everything else. Everything he had worked so hard for, for so long.

Yet he couldn't bear the thought of staying

away from her. Not when there was still so much to learn about her...

Orlando turned and strode away from Isabella's house. Florence was crowded, as always. Yet the feeling in the warm spring air wasn't the usual one of festive anticipation, when the season of parties and river pageants arrived, when Lent gave way to Easter. There was a thickness, a tension, one that Orlando could sense but couldn't quite decipher. It broke some of that heady joy from being with Isabella and reminded him sharply of the knife's edge his life really was.

He curled his fingers around the hilt of the dagger at his waist and turned towards narrower, rougher lanes away from the river. There, lounging with deceptive laziness beside a shade-dappled fountain, was the man he sought.

One of the guards he employed to keep an eye on this city, who had helped him rescue Isabella from the thieves, watched the crowd flow past as he pared his nails with a knife-point.

Orlando sat down beside him on the stone fountain ledge and he didn't even blink.

'What gossip do you hear of late?' Orlando asked. He crossed his booted ankles and studied the crowded square around them.

The guard shrugged. 'There is some discontent.'

Orlando gave a humourless laugh. 'That is like saying the sky is blue in Florence.'

'Some of the old families say the Medicis have got far above themselves.'

Orlando nodded. 'The Vespuccis? The Pazzis?'

The guard nodded. 'Them, and others.'

'Jacopo Pazzi has long made his peace with Lorenzo de Medici.'

'Perhaps old Jacopo has, but not his sons and grandsons, mayhap. The younger Jacopo has been ale-shot in many taverns lately, complaining of the Pazzi banks' losses to the Medici.'

And Matteo Strozzi was friends with the younger Pazzi, the two of them leaving a path of destruction through the brothels and taverns of the cities. Was Strozzi involved in the complicated tangle of Pazzi and Medici? Surely Strozzi was always spoiling for a fight, swaggering about with his guards and his hired bravos.

Perhaps there was a way Orlando could turn such resentments and quarrels to his own course. Use it to his advantage.

The image of Isabella flashed in his mind, her eyes full of wonder as she looked up at Botticelli's painting. After their kiss. Was she safe in the Strozzi house, amid these feuds she could not possibly understand? How could he keep her safe?

He pushed away the memory of her eyes and rose to his feet. She would be safe enough, no matter what happened. He would always see to that. He tossed a coin to the man.

'My thanks,' he said. 'Send me word when you hear any more. And have your men keep a close eye on the Strozzi house.'

The man nodded. The sun was high in the sky when Orlando emerged back on to one of the stone bridges over the Arno, but its heat seemed gone. He felt as cold as the depths of winter once again. As cold as the chapel where Maria Lorenza once lay.

Chapter Seven

Isabella dined alone with Caterina in her cousin's rooms, a quiet evening since Matteo had gone to supper at one of the Medici villas to meet a visiting cardinal. After the empty plates were cleared away and bowls of honeyed sweetmeats left, Caterina took up her lute.

She sat beside the window that looked down on the cobbled courtyard, her golden head bent over the polished wood as she strummed a quiet, bittersweet tune that seemed to fit perfectly with Isabella's own strange mood.

Isabella sat at the emptied table, turning her Venetian glass goblet between her fingers, letting the music wash over her as she remembered the days just past. Days unlike any other she had ever known, with a man she could not fathom.

She couldn't stop thinking about Orlando, seeing his face in her mind, the flash of his green eyes, the sudden sunlight of his smile. The way his lips felt on hers, so soft, so—so arousing.

She closed her eyes, seeing again the painting she had imagined of him. She'd teased him about portraying him as a court jester, but that would never do. There was nothing of the gambolling fool about him. The intense way he looked at the world, as if he saw all its hidden darkness…

Nay. He was brooding, watchful, waiting for the perfect moment to capture what he wanted.

Her eyes still closed, the painting took form in her mind like strokes of colour. Black, red, violet, streaks of sudden white. It would be dark, of course, with flashes of shimmering golden light as in Signor Botticelli's luminous work. Orlando on his towering ebony throne, his dark head leaning back as he surveyed his kingdom. One long, elegant hand curled into a fist, pale against the black velvet of his cloak, the other loosely wrapped around the ruby hilt of a dagger.

How would she paint the texture of the velvet, or the pleated linen draperies of the slave girls who would cluster at his feet? The rays of light streaming from the beautiful, light world above, so close yet so infinitely far away?

Most of all—how would she capture that elusive look in Orlando's beautiful eyes? The power, the beauty, the infinite sadness and longing that had so intrigued her there in the cathedral. She was drawn so close to him, even as her instincts told her she should run away. Protect herself. With him, she was far too vulnerable. She told him far more than she ever had anyone else. And she knew where such passion led when it was taken away, she had seen it with her own parents.

Half-aware, she traced the edge of her fingernail along the damask tablecloth as she imagined the scene. The sharp lines of the throne, the harsh, elegant angles of his face. The blurred edges of dark tapestries, the gleam of golden goblets. The black waves of his hair. Those sad eyes, so full of infinite emotions yet revealing nothing at all…

'My dear cousin,' Caterina said suddenly, her song dying away. 'I do hope your outings these last few days didn't tire you. Matteo said you were at the cathedral yesterday, and you were gone again this morning.'

Isabella's eyes flew open and she glanced up, startled. That phantom painting still clung to her mind, just as the real Orlando did. It was astonishing to be faced with the real, flesh-and-blood world. The luxurious chamber, draped in green-and-silver silk and fine tapestries. The crackling flames in the marble grate, the scent of wine and perfumed smoke from the gold burners. Her cousin's eyes, watching her too closely, as if she sensed Isabella's new secret.

But Isabella didn't want to talk about Orlando, not now. Maybe not ever. He seemed like a dream, like something precious and strange all for herself.

She flattened her hand against the table, feeling the embossed pattern of the cloth press into her skin. 'I wasn't tired at all. Florence is a most glorious city, I just want to see every bit of it.'

Caterina smiled gently. Her white fingers went back to strumming the lute strings. 'It's true, our city is beautiful and I want to share all I can with you, cousin. But Matteo said he found you alone at the church. You must be more careful.'

Isabella remembered how Matteo looked when he found her beneath the dome, surprised, cautious, and she felt again that flicker of disquiet. She told Caterina, as she had Matteo, that she did have a page with her. 'But I was enraptured with exploring. Is Florence so dangerous, then?' She knew it was. But the beauty almost overcame the fear.

A frown whispered over Caterina's smooth brow and she looked down at her lute. 'Florence always holds danger, especially among those who have powerful friends, as Matteo does. There are some who are jealous and who would wish him ill. Many undercurrents course here: alliances, hatreds, old quarrels. We must always be wary.'

Wary? Isabella suddenly wished she was back in the country, where life was so simple. She tried to laugh. 'Surely I am far too insignificant to be the focus of anyone's jealousies.'

Caterina smiled, but it looked sad. 'Oh, my dear. Florence may seem large and crowded, but everyone knows everyone here. You would be seen to be our kinswoman, especially after our visit to Botticelli. Apprentices are the greatest gossips of all. And if you hope to make a fine marriage…'

Isabella was startled by the word. 'Am I here to make a marriage?'

'I had hoped to find you a match among Matteo's friends. You are very pretty, Isabella, and intelligent and cultured. You would make a good wife for a wealthy banker or merchant.

And I do so love to play Cupid, with my sweet little arrows.'

Caterina wielded her lute like a bow. Isabella laughed, but inside her confusion and unease grew.

'Do you not wish to save one of those arrows for yourself, Caterina?' Isabella said.

Caterina shrugged and looked away, her face darkening like a rainy cloud. 'My health would not make me a suitable wife and I am happy living here with my brother and with my friends. Why should I give up so many admirers for one? And Matteo teases me that Signor Botticelli is my husband of the spirit. I love his work so very much!'

'So there is none to be jealous of you? Even Signor Botticelli?'

Caterina's smile returned and for the first time it reached her eyes. 'Alessandro does not—well, he does not admire women in that way. Not often.'

'Oh,' Isabella whispered. She knew of such things, of course. No educated child of a classical scholar could have missed it, the Trojans and Spartans and such. She should have sensed such in the way Botticelli looked at her and Caterina, with only the faintly removed spark of artistic awareness in his eyes.

Not like the look in Orlando's green eyes. That look that made Isabella feel hot and chilled all at the same time.

'Oh,' she said again and laughed.

'No one talks of such things aloud, of course,' Caterina said. 'But Matteo knows my reputation is safe at the studio, there are always other ladies there as Alessandro has so many muses.'

'And Giuliano de Medici?' Isabella said, the words escaping before she could capture them. 'Does he think you merely a friend?'

Caterina's smile flickered and she turned away to let the golden waves of her hair cover her face. 'Giuliano knows I can only be his friend. I have told him so many times. He only likes to flirt with me, tease me, as he does with all the ladies.'

Isabella was very sure that wasn't all there

was to the handsome Giuliano's feelings for her cousin. She'd seen the way he looked at Caterina, when he thought Caterina couldn't see. As if she was a goddess come to earth. But Caterina said naught could come of it.

Isabella couldn't help wondering what she herself would do if Orlando looked at *her* that way. She sipped at the last of her wine and dared to let herself imagine it.

'It grows late,' Caterina said quietly. 'We should retire, tomorrow will be very busy.'

'Oh, yes,' Isabella said, suddenly remembering what Giuliano had said. Remembering the matters of the real world beyond her romantic daydreams, the world of the beautiful city Caterina said held so many hidden dangers. 'A festival.'

'On the Prato. Giuliano will meet us at Botticelli's studio to escort us there,' Caterina said. 'It should be very merry! Dancing, music. Giuliano does like to put on a grand show...' Her voice suddenly faded and she turned away again. 'We must get our rest.'

She set aside her lute and led Isabella back to her own chamber, where she bid her good-night. Isabella found herself alone for the first time of that long, strange, amazing day. The candles were already lit in their gilded sconces, the bedclothes drawn back. The fine white sheets, sprinkled with lavender, beckoned, promising sweet dreams.

But despite the weariness of the long day, Isabella found she couldn't lie down just yet. She was seized by a strange restlessness. She pulled the new jewelled pins from her hair and let the heavy black waves fall over her shoulders as she went to the window.

She eased back a corner of heavy brocade curtains to peer down at the street. It was deep into the night now, the sky like black velvet overhead, with only the pearl-like dots of stars and a sliver of moon. In the *palazzo* across the way, the windows were lit up brightly, as if for a party. She could hear nothing from them. The street was quiet, emptied of the jostling bustle of the day, but somehow that light made her feel not so alone.

But through the thick glass of the windows she could see the heavy iron bars outside. Were they there to keep enemies out—or her in?

She ran her fingertips over the cool, damp glass and in her mind she saw again the image of the Underworld, and its dark lord. It trapped and attracted her all at the same time and she couldn't decide what was happening to her.

She jerked back from the window, letting the curtains swish back into place. Sleep was all she needed to clear her mind. Tomorrow she would be able to navigate this new world again.

Tomorrow, mayhap she would even see Orlando again. She didn't know if the prospect thrilled her—or frightened her to her very toes.

Lucretia walked with Orlando to the door of her *palazzo*, her hand light on his arm. From her salon, there was the echo of laughter, but Orlando couldn't feel a part of it tonight. Everything felt as if he watched it at a great distance.

'Must you leave so early, Orlando?' Lucretia said. 'We haven't even begun to truly make merry yet!'

Orlando laughed. 'I fear I am in no merry-making mood tonight, *bella*.'

'Who? You, who could always dance and drink 'til the dawn?'

'You do not need my help with that.'

She gently laid her palm against his cheek, her beautiful eyes full of worry. 'Does this have anything to do with your mysterious Isabella?'

Isabella. An image of her flashed through his mind, of her sweet smile as she looked up at him in the cathedral. The wonder of her kiss, so innocent, yet so passionate it carried him out of himself.

'Why would you think that?' he asked lightly.

Lucretia shook her head. 'She has something to do with the Strozzi, yes? And though you have never said why—you are far too good an actor even for me—I know you do not like them. Are you going to use this Isabella against them in some way?'

Orlando looked at her in shock. So devious. Why had he not thought such a thing? It would have been just like him, before. Before he saw Isabella. 'Surely you would not think me so ungallant?'

'You, Orlando? Ungallant? Never! 'Tis why my friends are all so in love with you. But Florence is so full of secrets. Everyone is using everyone else to their own ends. If she is a way to get closer to the Strozzi, who are so well guarded...'

Orlando felt an unaccountable anger burn inside of him. 'She is not,' he said shortly.

Lucretia studied him carefully for a long moment. 'Of course. But you could think of my words. Perhaps this Isabella could banish your demons, whatever they are.'

She kissed his cheek once more and pushed him off into the night.

Orlando was glad to be alone again in the darkness. Only at night did he feel he could drop the layers of his masks, let all his anger free. Tonight another of the demons Lucretia spoke of seemed to follow him. *Use Isabella,* it whispered. *She will get you near to the Strozzi.*

The man he had been only a few days ago would have certainly done it. Would have used any weapon at his disposal. But that was before he saw Isabella's smile.

She was a Strozzi, aye, but she was not of their dagger-sharp world. If he killed that innocence in her eyes…

Orlando kicked hard at a loose stone in the road. He had done villainous things in his past, true enough, but could he do such now?

He knew not where he was walking, yet somehow he found himself on the square where the Strozzi *palazzo* was the grandest structure. It was dark behind its thick stone walls, fortress-like in the night.

Yet the square itself was coming to life. Courtesans of a much lower order than Lucretia and her friends were gathering around the fountain, the moonlight shining on their bare shoulders, their laughter loud. One of them called out to Orlando, beckoning to him.

Maybe that was what he needed to exorcise this demon. To make him forget Isabella. Yet even as he smiled at the woman, started to answer her teasing words, something in him held him back.

He tossed her a coin and turned away, back to the Strozzi house. A flare of candlelight went up in one of the windows, and, as if his intense thoughts of her had conjured her, Isabella appeared behind the bars and the glass.

Her face was a pale blur, but the soft cloud of her loose black hair was unmistakable. She reached out and touched her fingertips to the glass, almost as if she saw him there. He opened his mouth to call out to her—then cursed himself for a fool. She could not see him, and even if she could he couldn't go to her.

If he was truly gallant, as Lucretia claimed, he would never see her again at all. Yet he couldn't turn away from the entrancing sight of her.

And Lucretia's words echoed in his mind. *Use her…*

The man he used to be would have. But now,

when he looked at her, he could see the truth of his own soul. He had changed, far too much. And that was a dangerous thing.

Chapter Eight

Isabella heard the revelry long before she could see it, a wild tangle of flutes and tambours, laughter, cries. She slowed down in sheer astonishment as they turned from the labyrinth of narrow lanes towards the meadow of the Prato, suddenly full of gladness at the sunny day.

The merriment, the glimpse of bright banners snapping in the breeze, the smell of roasting meats and cinnamon-spiced almonds—it all reminded her of festivals in the village at home, where music and parties cut into the sameness of everyday life and lifted everyone up.

As they stopped at the crest of a hill, Isabella glanced back over her shoulder to the stones and spires of the city. Her wide-brimmed velvet hat shaded her eyes from the sun that glittered in the clear turquoise sky. For an instant she fancied she could see Botticelli's studio, smell the tempera on the warm breeze. She remembered the half-finished painting on his easel, the scene of the magical garden. It felt as if she was about to step into it in truth.

'Isabella!' Caterina called. 'Hurry up, before all the strawberries have vanished.'

Isabella laughed and looked ahead to where Caterina walked with Giuliano. She hung on to his pearl-strewn velvet sleeve, their two beautiful heads bent together. 'We would never want that to happen!'

Caterina held out her free hand and Isabella hurried to take it. 'Just stay close to me, cousin, and all will be well,' Caterina whispered. But she did not smile as everyone else did. Instead she looked distinctly worried.

Isabella didn't know what could go wrong on such a glorious day, but there was no time to ask Caterina what concerned her. Giuliano led them onwards towards the party. He was just as handsome as Orlando in his own way, Isabella thought as she watched him. His face and figure were all that was perfection. And yet there was nothing intriguing behind his eyes, as there was with Orlando. No mystery, no depth.

The Prato was a vast green meadow near the banks of the Arno. Flowering trees and hedges blocked some of the sickly sweet smell from the river, adding splashes of pastel colours to the rolling green ground. But today the grass could hardly be seen for all the brightly clad revellers who crowded there amid the shade of silk pavilions.

Isabella followed Caterina through an archway of green vines and white flowers, and emerged from its shade into a sunlit, magical day. A garden of Venus.

Ladies in lustrous gowns of apricot, ochre-red, green, white, gold, their hair flowing free, twined with ribbons and flowers, danced in a lively, intricate circle on the grass. As their hands clasped, bells around their wrists tinkled, making them giggle. Around them moved a larger circle of men, even more elaborately dressed, with striped stockings and plumed caps. As Isabella watched, the two circles touched, meshed, then broke apart again. The music grew faster and faster, the colours blending together like a stained-glass window.

As Caterina and Giuliano stepped from the arch, applause broke out and they were soon surrounded by boisterous admirers.

Isabella was separated from them for a moment, lost in a swirling sea of jewels and feathers and perfumes. But she didn't mind. She searched each face, hoping she would see Orlando among them.

She'd dreamed of him last night, when she finally found her sleep. Wild images of his handsome face, his pale eyes. His hand beckoning to her, summoning her, only to vanish into the darkness. She didn't know if she wanted to find him, or if she should flee instead.

But he wasn't among the laughing crowds. She caught no glimpse of him at all, which made her heart sink a bit in disappointment.

'Isabella!' Caterina called. Isabella smiled, realizing she couldn't search for her Hades now. How could she even explain to her cousin her fascination for a man she had only seen a few times? A man who had kissed her and then vanished.

Giuliano and his boisterous friends led them to a pavilion that was set above the others on the highest hill, a beacon of shimmering white silk. Silver-and-green banners fluttered above it and soft silver cushions were scattered across the carpet underfoot and spilled out on to the grass. It was open on three sides, giving a perfect view of the dancing.

Isabella sat down on a plump cushion next to Caterina. As she removed her hat and smoothed the skirts of her new peach-and-gold silk gown, she tried not to stare at everything wide-eyed, like a country-bred child, but it was very difficult. It was all so very fascinating—the music, the fountains of wine, the damask-draped tables laden with delicacies.

Yet her Hades was not among them. She wondered, fancifully, if he lurked in his Underworld, listening to the human revels above him.

'What do you think of our rustic revels, Isabella?' Caterina asked.

Isabella laughed. 'Rustic? I have never seen such things on my father's farm.'

Caterina laughed, too, and her pale cheeks turned the faintest pink. 'Don't tell our young friends. They think their outdoor festivals are the perfect rendition of shepherds and shepherdesses. You see there? Simonetta even brought a lamb with her.'

Isabella frowned doubtfully as she watched a lady in purple satin and a pearl-beaded hair caul stroll past, leading a protesting lamb on a golden cord.

'We all need our little fantasies,' Caterina said. 'How else can we stand this world if not by self-deception?'

Isabella turned those words over in her mind. It was hard to think ill of the world on such a day, but Caterina had said there were things hidden there, things that could not be seen.

'Are you dispensing your golden wisdom, Caterina?' Giuliano asked, suddenly appearing back at Caterina's side, bearing a platter of glistening strawberries and grapes and a ewer of wine. More of his friends followed. Laughing, bowing, smiling. They were always smiling, unlike Orlando.

What was *their* self-deception?

'Are you in need of wisdom today, Giuliano?' Caterina said. 'I fear I have nothing to help you.'

'On the contrary.' Giuliano knelt beside her and offered her a perfect, plump, ruby-red strawberry. 'You, my beauteous Caterina, have everything.'

Caterina took the fruit and held it up. Its redness was bright, almost sinister against the white silk. 'I was merely warning Isabella to be wary of young men bearing flattery. Especially on a beautiful spring day, when the light can so easily dazzle.'

Cold disquiet touched Isabella as she studied the light-washed scene beyond their shaded pavilion. Was she merely dazzled by it all? Blinded by her sudden entrance into a world so very different from her own? By the outward beauty of it all?

She watched a couple parade past, laughing together, a vivid peacock pair in blue and green. They twirled in a sudden, spontaneous dance step and it made Isabella dizzy to watch. They seemed happy, careless, as everyone else did. As if no ugliness or sadness could ever touch them, not in a joyous place like Florence.

Isabella closed her eyes, suddenly confused. She didn't feel like herself at all. In the flashing shadows behind her eyes, she saw an image of him. Orlando. She saw him again as he was there in the cathedral, when they were alone together high above the bright marble world.

With him, she felt as if she caught a glimpse of deeper truths. A flash of raw, vivid emotion caught like the glint of a drawn sword in his eyes. But then it had been gone, lost in the laughter everyone here hid behind. And he had vanished himself, into the crowds of the cathedral.

Was he even real?

A burst of laughter broke over the moment of Isabella's disquiet, the moment of her yearning for something she couldn't even name. She opened her eyes to see Caterina shaking her head at Giuliano's teasing. The studied laughter, the smell of strawberries and white flowers, the strong wine—it was suddenly all too much. She needed some fresh air.

Isabella pushed herself to her feet, careful to keep a smile on her lips. 'I will return in a moment, Caterina.'

Caterina glanced up at her, surprise in her eyes. 'Is something amiss, Cousin?'

'Not at all. I just need a—a moment,' Isabella answered, hoping perhaps Caterina would think she meant something rather indelicate and wouldn't question further.

It seemed to work. Caterina nodded and went back to Giuliano, and Isabella ducked out of the pavilion and into the sunlight.

She didn't know where she was going, she
only knew she had to get away, to find some
place quiet where her whirling thoughts could
be still. She held the hem of her fine new gown
above the damp grass and found a pathway that
wound around the edge of the meadow.

Soon, the sounds of music and laughter were
only a blur behind her. She climbed up the slope
of a hill to find the shade of a grove of cypress
trees at the crest. She leaned against the rough
bark of the trunk, trying to catch her breath
as she stared at the city beyond. From there,
even the great, rose-red dome of the cathedral
looked small.

'I see you are hiding away again.'

The words were quiet, touched with hidden
laughter, but they made her heart leap. She spun
around, startled and suddenly joyful, to find
Orlando standing near the mate to her shelter-
ing tree.

His stance was careless, nonchalant, one hand
resting on the tree, the other loosely wrapped
around the jewelled hilt of the dagger at his belt.

He wore black again, velvet and silk touched with flashes of dark blue that brought out the glints in his dark hair. But the look in his eyes was not brooding, as it had been at the cathedral. There was a sparkle there, a touch of teasing laughter that made her want to laugh, too. Before she knew what she was doing, she took a step closer to him.

''Tis you who always appear so suddenly, *signor*,' she said. 'And disappear just as quickly. I begin to think you are a spirit.'

'Surely no spirit could do this, *signorina*.' His hand suddenly reached out and took hers, his fingers warm and strong over hers.

Isabella stared in wonder at their fingers entwining. The sun-browned, slightly callused elegance of his; her own pale, paint-spattered skin. The glint of an amethyst ring on his finger. She seemed to see it all in detail, like a painting, yet there was no cool distance. She could feel every emotion vividly.

'I have never met a spirit, in truth,' she murmured. 'But I would wager it would not feel like this.'

His hand tightened on hers, binding her to him. She wanted to be even closer. 'How does it feel, Isabella?'

She couldn't tell him how it really felt when he touched her—as if she was lighter than air, free from the earth and soaring into the sky. As if she wanted to laugh and sob all at the same time. As if she wanted *everything*, only with him.

'It makes me feel as if I could never get enough of it,' she said.

His eyes darkened and his teasing smile faded as he studied her intently.

Isabella's legs went weak under her and she swayed towards him. He held on to her tightly and it was as if he was all there was in the world, him and his wondrous eyes looking at her as if she was all he could see as well. That they were alone.

No one had ever looked at her like that, as if they could see right down to her soul.

She slowly reached up and touched his cheek. His skin was warm and taut as sun-bronzed satin, roughened by whiskers along the carved line of his jaw. She ran her fingertips over his lips, which parted slightly as if she startled him. They were so surprisingly soft…

He lowered his head and touched those lips to hers.

It was slow and soft as he brushed his mouth back and forth over hers, pressing tiny touches to her lower lip. Those slow caresses ignited something deep inside of her, some need she never even knew was there and yet now it was the most urgent thing in the world. She curled her hands into the soft velvet of his doublet and held on to him as she tumbled down into a new, magical world.

He groaned deep in his throat, and suddenly the kiss changed, became deeper, more frantic. When she gasped, he slid inside, his tongue twining with hers.

It was so very intimate. She could taste him, the sweet darkness of him. Her arms slid around him and through the layers of velvet and leather she could feel the shift of his taut muscles, the strength of his body. Through the sparkling haze that had fallen over her senses, she felt his hand slide down her back and pull her up against him.

His lips slid from hers, along her cheek, tracing her skin as if he wanted to learn her. He nipped at a spot just below her ear that was shockingly sensitive. She sighed with the pleasure, which felt like a ripe summer fruit bursting, sweet and sensual, and she needed more.

But there were voices echoing below their secret place and she realized where they were. The scandal she could bring on Caterina if someone saw them. He seemed to realize it, too, and tilted his head back. He drew in a ragged breath.

Isabella closed her eyes and leaned her forehead against Orlando's shoulder as she tried to catch her breath. As she waited for the world to stop tilting around her. She could hear his heart beat in her ears as if it was her own, its pattern swift as the drums in the distance.

At least he felt it, too, she thought with a smile as she heard him drag in a deep, unsteady breath. At least she was not alone in these sudden, wild yearnings.

Could it be—was it…that she was falling in love with him?

The thought struck her like a sudden cold, stinging rain shower on a summer's day. *Nay!* She could not be falling in love, not just like that with a man she had just met. Not after the pain she knew always came after love. She didn't live in a sonnet. Such loves were not for mere mortals, especially not for people who thought themselves dull and sensible as she did. It was just…

What *was* it?

She stared up at him in complete bewilderment. How very handsome he was, not like a human at all, with his hair tousled over his brow and a half smile on his lips. His eyes were narrowed as he looked down at her.

'Isabella,' he said softly, her name rich and sweet in his deep, roughened voice. She'd never heard it said quite like that before. He reached up and gently touched her cheek, a whisper of a caress. His fingers were warm on her skin and she wanted to lean into him. To hold on to him and never let go.

Such longings frightened her. She stepped back away from the touch that so confused her. His hand fell to his side and he frowned.

'Isabella, what is amiss?' he asked.

She shook her head. 'I—nothing is amiss. I just realized I have been away from my cousin too long. She will be looking for me.'

'She will be busy with all her suitors,' he said and she could tell he tried to tease her, to bring back some of the lightness of that perfect day, the laughter of their dance. 'We have time.'

Isabella wanted their dance back, too. In those few moments she'd felt so glorious, so perfectly happy. But, like so much in Florence, it was surely an illusion. She didn't want to be lost in it.

'I should go,' she whispered. She whirled around, but he reached out and caught her hand before she could flee. His clasp was gentle, yet she feared she couldn't break free.

'Forgive me, Isabella,' he said and she heard the most solemn truth in his voice, just as she had when she had so briefly glimpsed his sadness at the cathedral. 'I never meant insult to you. I forgot myself for a moment. I have never met anyone quite like you before.'

She glanced back at him over her shoulder and he gave her a rakish smile. His eyes were so brilliant, like emeralds in the sunlight. 'I am not insulted, I promise you. And I have never met anyone like you, either.'

His smile turned hopeful. 'Then may I see you again?'

She did want that; she longed for it too much. She nodded.

'When?' he said.

'I don't know,' she answered, growing more desperate to back away from his touch. Or she wouldn't be able to leave at all. 'I don't know what will happen next any longer. Once, I knew so well what every day would bring. Now…'

Now, she knew less and less with every moment that passed.

He nodded and let her go. 'I will watch, to make sure you reach your cousin safely,' he said. 'We will meet again soon, Isabella.'

She spun around and hurried back down the hill towards the noisy crowds, the cluster of pavilions. Only once did she look back, but she couldn't see Orlando any longer. He had vanished, just as he had in the cathedral. Yet she was sure she felt the heavy heat of his gaze.

She moved more slowly into the party, past ladies playing with their lapdogs and giggling together, dancers spinning in ever more wild circles, a priest lurching past drunkenly.

She could see Caterina's pavilion in the distance and glimpsed a flash of her cousin's purple gown. Caterina was watching a cluster of men play at bocce on the grass, including Giuliano de Medici. He had stripped to his fine white lawn shirt to toss the ball towards the pins, surely only to impress Caterina.

As she made her way past a cluster of men around one of the wine fountains, Isabella heard someone mutter a low curse and something about the Medici. How they should be wary.

Startled, she slowed her steps, trying to hear more. Who were those men who muttered so darkly about the Medici? Some of those hidden enemies Caterina spoke of?

Isabella glanced at the embroidered badges on their blue-and-gold doublets. The twin dolphins of the Pazzi family.

'Ah, now here is a pretty maid, come to relieve us of hearing of the perfidious Medici again!' One of the younger men suddenly reached out towards Isabella as she edged past him. She managed to twirl away and his grasp slid off her silk sleeve.

She rushed away, his drunken laughter following her. When she was at a safe distance, she looked back. They still leaned against each other, glaring at Giuliano and his friends.

She wasted no more time in making her way back to Caterina. She found she was shaking and was most grateful to sink down on to a cushion and take a goblet of wine from one of the pages.

Caterina smiled at her. Her cheeks were pink from laughing at Giuliano's antics and luckily she didn't seem to have noticed how long Isabella was gone.

'Is anything amiss, cousin?' Caterina said. 'You look a bit flustered.'

'Do you know those men there?' Isabella asked. She gestured to the group near the fountain. The young man who had tried to grab her hand had found a more willing lady, who giggled up at him. A cardinal had joined them, an even younger man who seemed too small for his heavy red robes, or for the overflowing golden goblet in his hand.

A frown whispered over Caterina's lips. 'The

Pazzi? They are one of the wealthiest families in Florence. Another banking family.'

Isabella remembered hearing about the Pazzi family, an old, wealthy family with many connections across Italy. 'Bankers to the pope himself?'

'Aye. The papal account was rightfully that of the Medici bank, until this new pope decided he felt otherwise. That small blond man is Francesco Pazzi, while the cardinal is the pope's nephew, Signor Riario.'

'I see,' Isabella said slowly. Now their muttered words about Giuliano made sense.

'Did they bother you, Isabella?' Caterina said, her voice concerned.

Isabella shook her head. 'Nay. One of them tried to flirt with me when I walked past, but I think he was merely ale-shot.'

Giuliano gave a shout as he overshot his aim with the bocce ball and nearly toppled over. Caterina smiled indulgently. 'Many are today, I fear. If you were hurt…'

Isabella shook her head. The last thing she

wanted was to mar this day with a brawl. 'I can look after myself.' Usually, anyway. She was not quite so sure any longer.

Caterina turned back to the game and Isabella surveyed the crowd as she sipped her wine. Orlando was nowhere to be seen. She hadn't expected he would, but still...

Still, she had foolishly hoped.

Chapter Nine

The *palazzo* was silent as Isabella slipped out of her chamber into the corridor. It was deep into the night, but candles were lit in the sconces, casting their glow into the mysterious darkness. Their hiss and flicker seemed to be the only life in the perfect stillness of the house.

Caterina had retired after the party, her face white and strained with fatigue, and the servants disappeared after bringing Isabella her supper. Matteo had never come home at all. The last Isabella saw of him was when he reeled away from the Prato with his equally wine-besotted friends, singing a bawdy song.

Isabella knew she should sleep as well. It had been such a long day, filled with sunshine and wine and such a wild swirl of emotions. She hadn't seen Orlando again, even though she had searched for him through the dancers and the games. Even though she could not forget his kiss, the way it made her feel, so wild and exultant, so full of longing.

As if she had been searching and searching for so long, looking for that one perfect moment, and then it was upon her. It had been so *right*. But now it was gone, leaving her confused and alone once again.

So, aye, she *should* be sleeping. Forgetting everything in dreams. But she couldn't lie still, couldn't quiet her thoughts. The spring night was warm and her chamber felt too close. She remembered Mena telling her about a large terrace on the top floor of the *palazzo*. A large, shaded landing where the family could watch processions on the street below, or where the servants could hide for a bit of purloined wine. Isabella thought maybe she could sit there for a time, find some fresh air and watch the city that had so beguiled her.

She had quickly tugged on one of her simple dresses from home and left her hair loose, freed from its elaborate braids and curls. The fine silks and jewels from the party were left behind. She wrapped a thin shawl around her shoulders as she made her way up the narrow back staircase. She encountered no one. It felt as if the house was indeed deserted.

She found the landing off a small antechamber at the top of the house. Her shoes clicked on the flagstone floor as she tiptoed over to lean on the railing and study the street below. Unlike the *palazzo*, Florence was not completely silent for the night. In the distance, she could hear the echo of music and light once again flickered in the house across the square.

Isabella leaned down to rest her chin on her palm, closing her eyes as she let the night wash over her. She thought of Orlando, the way his hands felt as she danced with him, his kiss. She had never imagined a kiss could feel like that…

A sudden, sharp crack made her eyes fly open, startled. She stood up straight just in time to see a flare of fireworks shoot over the tiled roofs of the city. Red, white, green, sparkling and shimmering before it disappeared into the night sky.

Astonished by the sudden burst of beauty, she laughed when a plume of silver shot into the sky amid the drifts of smoke. It was like so many things that had happened to her since she came to Florence—unexpected, unlooked for and entirely amazing. A whole new world of possibilities opening up where anything could happen.

Overcome by the flash of joy, Isabella spun around in a wide circle, her arms outflung as if she would dance. Her shawl fell to the floor and the wind brushed over her shoulders, catching at her hair.

She whirled to a stop, gasping for breath as she found herself looking down at the street again. Only now it was not deserted. A man in a hooded cloak stood across the way, his shadowed face turned up to watch her balcony.

Isabella's sudden wild burst of joy turned to

cold fear. She remembered all Caterina's warnings of the hidden dangers of Florence and felt foolish for letting herself forget again. She fell back a step, intending to flee, but something stopped her. Something about that man, about his tall figure, the way he stood…

He reached up to push back the hood and the torchlight from the street flickered over his face. It was Orlando who watched her, Orlando who had come there. To find her?

Isabella could hardly dare hope he *had* come for her. Perhaps he was merely passing, pausing to watch some hoydenish girl leap about. And yet—she did remember that kiss. The way he was so gentle, so sweet, until everything caught fire. The way his heart pounded, just as hers did.

She edged back carefully to the railing to stare down at him, unable to leave. 'Orlando?' she called.

'Don't be frightened, Isabella, please,' he answered. He stepped closer, his face turned up to her perch. He gave her the smile that always made her heart beat faster.

'What are you doing here?' she said, holding her breath as she wondered what his answer would be.

'It was foolish of me, I know,' he said. He smiled, a rakish, white grin that gleamed in the torchlight and made her smile too. 'But I wanted to see if I could catch a glimpse of you. The gods have smiled on me tonight.'

Isabella laughed, delighted beyond measure that he wanted to see her. 'How did you know I lived here?'

'I know much about Florence, Isabella, and I would share it with you if you would let me.'

Share it with her—and then vanish again? Yet Isabella found she was so happy, almost giddy, to see him that his mysteriousness mattered not at all. Not now. He seemed such a part of her joyous mood.

'I suppose you even ordered the fireworks, just so I could see the city by night,' she teased.

''Twas the Medici, I am sure. They like to

display their wealth at every opportunity. But I will take the credit, if it pleases you.'

'Your being here pleases me,' Isabella admitted, forgetting all caution.

'Shall I come up, then?' he said. 'Or shall I shout here in the street until your neighbours are all roused and there is a great scandal?'

'You cannot come up here,' she said with a laugh. 'I doubt you can fly.' He was Hades after all, not Icarus. Yet tonight he looked too young and teasing to be god of the Underworld. How quickly he changed with every moment. How much he intrigued her.

'I don't have to build wings,' he said. He suddenly leaped up, grabbing a skein of looping ivy that hung from the stone wall.

Isabella watched in astonishment as he used the ivy as a rope to pull himself upwards. 'Nay!' she cried with a jolt of fear. 'You will fall.'

'How little faith you have in me, fair Isabella,' he said lightly. He reached a lower, smaller balcony, and leaped on to its railing.

'I have faith you are not a bird,' she said. She

couldn't quite breathe as he continued to make his way upwards.

'Nor am I the soft city-bred fool you seem to think me,' he said. He wasn't out of breath at all. 'I grew up at my father's country villa, swimming, rowing…'

'Climbing?'

'Aye, that, too. I also practised swordplay, wrote poetry. I am a man of many talents.'

'So I am beginning to see,' Isabella said. She thought she could be fascinated by every aspect of him for a very long time. That was the very thing she feared most.

At last, he caught the railing of her own balcony and swung himself up and over. He landed lightly, almost soundlessly, like a cat, and grinned at her as he stood up straight.

'Do I get a reward for my brave exploits?' he said.

He held out his arms and Isabella couldn't help herself. She ran into them, laughing. His arms slid around her, drawing her tight against him just as she had wanted ever since their sun-lit dance.

'Is a kiss enough reward?' she whispered.

In answer, he pulled her even closer, his mouth came down over hers and his tongue slid against hers. She opened for him, letting him in, meeting him eagerly. She loved when he kissed her and this happened, when everything else disappeared and there was only the magic of how he made her feel. He tasted of wine and mint, of the dark richness of the night.

His hand slid down her back as the kiss grew deeper. The night wind was chilly, but she could only feel his heat. His hard hand cupped her backside through her thin gown, shockingly, wonderfully, and he pulled her up into his body. She moaned against his mouth.

He lifted her up high against him and swung her around until she was braced against the stone wall of the *palazzo*. She felt free suddenly, as if she flew free, and she dared to wrap her legs around his waist, holding him close to her. She could feel the hardness of his desire through his doublet and tights, and it sent a primal thrill through her. He wanted her just as she wanted him. She tilted back her head and laughed out of sheer joy.

His lips slid down her arched neck, the tip of his tongue dipping into the hollow at the base of her throat. Her pulse pounded there, frantic with need. Something deep inside of her, something dark and primitive, called out for him.

He caressed the softness of her breast through her gown, his thumb brushing over her aching nipple. 'Isabella, *cara*. I need…'

'I know,' she gasped. She threaded her fingers through his tousled hair and drew his mouth back to her skin. She shivered as he kissed her throat, his breath warm against her, and cried out as his hand touched her.

'You are so beautiful,' he said. 'I've never known anyone like you.'

He kissed her again and she heard the mingling of their harsh breath, his incoherent words. The city far below was forgotten, there was only him. Only his kiss.

His hand slid lower, over her hip, her bent thigh, until he grasped her skirt in his fist. He drew it up, his palm smoothing over her bare skin. His touch on her naked flesh was wondrous. She held on to him blindly, wrapping herself closer around him.

'I want you so much, *bella*,' he said. 'But I can't…not here. Like this…'

A cold disappointment flooded over her, yet she knew he was right. This wasn't the place, the time. Surely he felt something for her, something like what she felt for him? Surely this was not all there would be for them. It couldn't be. Not when her whole world had changed because he had appeared in it.

She opened her eyes and studied his handsome face as she caught her breath. He stared down at her, a strange blend of pleasure and pain in his eyes. Regret?

Nay, there could be no regret. Not for something like this.

'Yes,' she said. 'I will see you soon enough, Orlando. But that you came here tonight…'

He smiled, that flash of darkness vanishing, and he bent his head to kiss her again, quickly. Softly. 'We will see each other again, *cara*. I vow it.'

Orlando stood concealed just beyond the corner of the house across from the Strozzi *palazzo*, watching the light glowing from the window of the chamber he knew was Isabella's. He knew he should go. That he should turn his back on that cursed house and never look back. Never see Isabella again.

But some powerful, irresistible force held him where he was. He couldn't look away from that light. It was as if he stared at the very last beacon in a bleak, black world.

And that was exactly what Isabella was. A glimmer of pure light, a shining, silvery, dancing star, in the waste of his life.

He braced his arm against the cold stone wall, thinking of the heat of Isabella in his arms. The glorious burst of passionate life that broke over him. When he was with her, he felt none of the taint of his past, of the mistakes he had made, the people he had hurt. Life felt so new when he was with her, so full of hope.

It was an illusion, perhaps the cruellest he'd ever known, but it was also intoxicating. He wanted more and more of it, more of *her*.

That was what drew him to her house tonight. Even as he knew it was the last place he should be, he was pulled there. And when he saw her on the terrace, as if she waited just for him…

He had to go to her. Surely he would have died in that moment if he couldn't feel her in his arms. And when he kissed her at last—it was as if he slipped into a heaven he did not deserve.

And now the pain was ten times greater. He saw what he could have had in her—and he knew it was all much too late.

Lucretia had been right. Isabella got him into the home of the Strozzi. But the softness of her eyes wounded him.

He drove his fist into the hard stone of the wall, trying to create a new pain to chase the ache in his heart away. But the physical pain was no escape, just as he couldn't find escape in drink or other women. Isabella was what drew him in now. Isabella was what he wanted.

And she was exactly what he could not have.

He heard a noise from behind him, faint but growing louder, a wild tangle of raucous laughter and shouts. Orlando pressed his back to the wall, his fist instinctively closing around the dagger at his belt.

A group of young men, obviously ale-shot, tumbled into the narrow lane. They were shoving each other, laughing, passing a flask between them. One of them was Orlando's friend Paolo, a man he often saw at Lucretia's salon.

'Orlando!' Paolo shouted. 'Where have you been hiding of late? All the tavern wenches are desolate. I can't handle all of them by myself.'

Orlando's hand loosened on his dagger but did not fall away. No one could really be trusted in Florence, even—especially—ones who called themselves friends.

'I have had much business to attend to,' he answered.

'Business? Pah!' Paolo cried. He stumbled closer to Orlando and clapped him on the shoulder. Everyone else tumbled after him, loud and clamorous, the strong odour of wine hovering around them. 'Pleasure comes before all, surely. We are going to Celeste's house now. Come with us.'

Orlando shook his head. Such places as Celeste's, where once he buried his anger and sorrow, held no attractions at all. Not after Isabella and the sweet laughter he found in her arms. Not after he glimpsed what life *could* be like.

But he couldn't have Isabella. Not really, not for ever.

He looked back to her window. It was dark now. Isabella was gone.

And so was his old life. Perhaps he could not have Isabella. But he could try to be a man worthy of her. She had given him that.

'Nay,' he told Paolo. 'Not tonight. I have other matters to attend to…'

Chapter Ten

'I found out a bit about your mysterious Isabella,' Lucretia said as she walked with Orlando along the Arno. She had drawn her silk veil close against the springtime sun, but he could see the edge of her teasing smile.

'You work quickly, Lucretia.'

'Of course, *caro*. Information is of no use to a woman like me when it is stale. But I fear there is little of interest to know. She doesn't seem like your usual sort at all.'

His usual sort. Orlando had to laugh wryly when he thought of some of the women in his past. Sophisticated, elegant Lucretia had been the exception to bawdier, darker courtesans, tavern maids, bored older ladies looking for diversion just as he was. Women who could make him forget Maria Lorenza, even if it was just for an hour.

Nay—Isabella was assuredly nothing like any of them. She wasn't like anyone he had ever known at all, an intriguing mix of artistry and innocence. And last night, when he held her in his arms and buried his face in the perfume of her hair, he felt as he never had before. He felt—clean. Free.

Happy.

Orlando shook his head. He had little memory of how it felt to be happy. When he was a child, mayhap, when his mother and Maria Lorenza were alive and life seemed as a perpetually warm summer. Before things turned cold and dark, and all he could think of was death and revenge. Isabella drove all that away when he was with her. She made the world seem fresh and new again, as he saw it through the artistry of her eyes.

He knew that it all came much too late. His course was set and he could not alter it. He had given his vow to Maria Lorenza. Fate seemed determined to make a joke of him, sending Isabella into his life right at this moment.

He sensed Lucretia watching him closely and realized he had been silent too long. He gave her a careless smile, but he could tell she wasn't fooled.

'So tell me what you have heard, fair Lucretia,' he said.

She shrugged, the pale gold silk of her gown rippling in the light. 'As I said, there is not much to know. Either she is as dull and blameless as a saint, or most adept at hiding her secrets. She is kin to the Strozzi, after all.'

Orlando felt a flash of anger to be reminded she was connected to the Strozzi. Another sharp joke of fate. 'She is not like them.'

'Ah. A saint, then.'

He remembered how her arms held him so close, how her lips opened so eagerly beneath his as she met his kisses with the fire of a raw, untamed passion. He smiled despite himself. 'Not that, either.'

'If she can make you smile like that, Orlando, then she is deceptively intriguing,' Lucretia said with a laugh. 'It seems her long-dead mother was sister to the father of Matteo and Caterina Strozzi. But she was married off when she was a girl to the scholar, Signor Spinola, and seldom returned to Florence. Signor Spinola is well-known among my friends for his writings. He corresponds with many philosophers and artists, yet few have actually met him. He never leaves his villa. But Mario did spend a few days with him last year, and I saw Mario yesterday. I asked about the Spinolas.'

Mario was young and handsome, though known to be rather shy and devoted to his books. Had he met Isabella when he visited her father? Talked to her, walked with her through the country hills?

Orlando almost laughed at himself. He had no right to be jealous of anyone Isabella talked to. Indeed, jealousy was an emotion foreign to him. But he found he could cheerfully strangle Mario if Isabella laughed with him.

'And what did Mario say?' he asked tightly.

'Much of the father's great wisdom, but almost nothing of the daughter,' Lucretia answered. 'Just that she liked to paint and seemed a good companion to her father. It seems that was why she came to Florence, to be companion to Signorina Caterina until she returns to health, if she ever does. I would wager her cousins wish to make a match for her as well.'

Orlando frowned. 'Is a match known?'

Lucretia shook her head. 'Not yet. I heard she is pretty enough to gather some admirers, though sadly her hair is dark and she has no large fortune. The Strozzi will use every tool they have to make alliances. If you have taken a liking to her…'

'I was merely curious about her,' he lied.

Lucretia laughed. 'I know you better than that, Orlando. You have never asked about a respectable lady before and the way you try to conceal your interest tells me there is much to this.'

He smiled ruefully. 'Am I too obvious now?'

'Only to me. No one else knows anything about you at all. That's why all my female friends are so intrigued by you. I don't know the nature of your dislike for the Strozzi—this city is filled with old quarrels. But if you admire Isabella Spinola, perhaps she could be a way to reconcile—'

'Nay,' Orlando cut her off, an image of Maria Lorenza's white, dead face flashing in his mind. 'That is not possible.'

Lucretia shrugged. 'If you say so. Men can be so very single-minded. If I hear anything else about your pretty artist, I will write to you.'

'Write to me?'

The bells from the cathedral began to peal the hour, a slow, deep sound that echoed over the tiled roofs and across the sparkling waves of the river. Lucretia tilted her head as if to listen.

'I am leaving Florence for my country villa,' she said.

Orlando was surprised. 'Leaving the city? You?'

'It is nearly the penitential season, time for reflection. I feel the need for some fresh air.' She looked up at him, her beautiful face suddenly solemn. 'I sense something strange is coming to our fair city, Orlando *caro*.'

'What have you heard?' he asked. He thought of what his contact had told him, of the Pazzi and their grudges. The strange tension in the air of late.

'Nothing specific. But there is much anger, towards the Medici in particular. They have taken so much from so many. And now they entertain a cardinal who is the pope's nephew— when everyone knows the pope hates them. I do not like it. So I will retreat for Lent.'

Orlando frowned. If Lucretia was leaving the city, something truly must be in the air. Something that could hurt Isabella? He could never let that happen. And yet surely he was the one who could hurt her the most.

Lucretia gently touched his cheek. 'Do be careful, Orlando.'

He smiled at her, hoping she did not see the

turmoil that caught at him inside. 'I am always careful.'

'Not always, I think. And passion can make fools of us all sometimes.'

She took his arm and they continued along the river's edge in silence, the toll of the bells the only sound.

'Isabella, what is so fascinating out that window?' Caterina called.

Isabella laughed at herself, for she couldn't help but peek out the window every few minutes. She glanced back at Caterina, who was working at her embroidery. 'Nothing at all. I just can't seem to sit still today.'

And she couldn't stop thinking about Orlando, as he had been last night on the moonlit terrace. Kissing her, holding her. It had been like a dream, and she still felt giddy with it all. Every tall, dark-haired gentleman who walked past made her heart quicken, but it was never him.

The sleepless night was making her fuzzy-headed.

Caterina gave her an indulgent smile. 'It is the party yesterday. I know the feeling—the music won't leave you. Or perhaps one of Matteo's handsome friends caught your eye?'

Isabella felt her cheeks grow warm and she turned to look out the window again. 'Not at all.'

Caterina laughed. 'Come now, cousin! I know the signs of a new infatuation. There are many charming men in Florence and it would be entirely natural, desirable even, if you liked one.'

Liked one? Was that what her feelings were? Infatuation. Perhaps it was. An infatuation that would fade away as she became more experienced and met more men.

Yet she feared that wasn't what it was at all. It was not something that would just fade away. When she looked at him, she felt as she did when she looked at a painting. So carried away by the beauty of it she wanted to cry.

'No one has caught my eye in that way,

Caterina. And I'm sure Matteo's friends wouldn't consider me that way, either.'

'Of course they would! You are lovely. And a connection with Matteo would be a fine thing for any Florentine family.'

Isabella was startled, but she suddenly realized she shouldn't be. Caterina had mentioned marriage the first day Isabella arrived. A connection for family…

And who really was Orlando? A man who vanished like a ghost.

'You can examine them closer at church tomorrow,' Caterina said. 'It is a holy day at the cathedral. Everyone in Florence will be there. Especially with the pope's nephew Cardinal Riario officiating. You must wear your new blue satin.'

'Caterina—' Isabella began, only to break off. What could she say? This was a new world, a new dance, and she was just beginning to learn the steps. All she really knew was who she wanted to partner her in this strange pavane.

'Yes,' she said. 'I look forward to it.'

Chapter Eleven

'*Pange, lingua, gloriosi! Corporis mysterium…*'

Isabella followed Caterina into the vast space of Santa Maria del Fiore, pausing inside the great bronze doors to cross herself with holy water. She stared at the scene before her, struck by its strange beauty. It looked like a colourful gathering in one of Signor Botticelli's otherworldly canvases.

On the day she climbed to the choir loft with Orlando, the church had been crowded but had still felt empty, echoing. Today, people were packed in closely along the nave, shifting about, whispering together, laughing behind fans. The blur of their fine clothes and glowing jewels made them blend into the stained-glass windows that cast shards of brilliant light over the inlaid floors and pale stone walls.

Caterina took her arm and drew her into the crowd. People called out greetings to Caterina and she paused to kiss cheeks, to smile and laugh. She had looked pale, listless since the party on the Prato, but today her cheeks were flushed as pink as her pearl-studded gown.

Isabella was happy to see her cousin look so happy again, yet she knew so little of Florence gossip she had nothing to add to the conversation. She inhaled deeply of the mingled scents of incense and expensive perfumes—rose, jasmine and violet—and studied the scene around her. She wished she had her sketchbook, to work it all into a painting later.

All of Florence seemed to have put on their very finest to come to church that day. After all, it was a holy day and a cardinal who was the pope's own nephew was to preside. Every great family was arrayed there.

But not yet the Medici. Isabella went up on tiptoe to examine the faces around her. Lorenzo de Medici and his brother Giuliano were not yet there, nor was Matteo. Her cousin had not been home much of late. Caterina had said Giuliano was ill with a leg injury after the Prato, and Matteo and their other friends had to entertain the visitors. Yet surely they would appear for such an important Mass?

Nor did she see Orlando and her heart sank a little with disappointment. She dared not admit to herself just how much she wanted to glimpse his face.

Above Caterina's whispers with her friends, the cathedral was alive with sound. The chanting of the choir, the tolling of bells from the tower, the clink of swords in their scabbards, the stiff rustle of fine fabrics, the clatter of jewelled bracelets. Then a hush rolled over the crowd as the bronze doors opened and Lorenzo de Medici and his retainers came in.

The mythically powerful head of the Medici was certainly not a handsome man, Isabella thought as she watched him stride to his place alongside the gilded altar rail. Yet she would love to sketch him. His face was pockmarked, dominated by a flattened nose and a heavy, jutting jaw. Yet every bit of him fairly vibrated with a crackling energy, a vivid awareness of everything around him.

Giuliano followed, sumptuously dressed, but a bit pale, leaning heavily on the shoulder of the same slight, young blond man Isabella had seen at the Prato. Francesco Pazzi, Caterina had called him. Giuliano went in the opposite direction from his brother and disappeared into the crowd near the doors.

That seemed to be the signal for the Mass to begin. To the peal of dozens of silver altar bells, the pope's cardinal nephew appeared in his scarlet robes, preceded by dozens of acolytes swinging their censers.

'*Corporis mysterium…*'

Isabella tried to pay attention to the service, to not look for Orlando again. But she couldn't help but search the faces once more. Every bit of her mind seemed to be focused on seeing him again, as it had been much too often of late.

A bell tolled again, and the cardinal raised the Host over his head. Suddenly, the incense-scented hush of the church was broken by a rough shout.

'People and liberty!' someone screamed.

'What is happening?' Caterina cried, clutching at Isabella's arm.

Isabella could see nothing past the bodies packed around her. Panic seemed to break over the crowd like a tidal wave, sweeping aside the peace of that holy place. People scattered in every direction, screaming, crying, tripping over each other. She felt closed in, trapped. Her whole body seemed frozen to the spot.

'The dome is falling!' someone shouted.

Isabella glanced up, shocked. She could see nothing of the soaring dome from her place in the nave, but she didn't hear any crack or crash of masonry. Only the panicked screams of the fleeing congregation.

She held on to Caterina and strained to see anything that was happening, any way to get away. Cardinal Riario still stood at the altar, still as a statue, and she glimpsed Lorenzo de Medici's back as his friends pushed him into the sacristy and swung the heavy doors closed behind them.

Frantic, Isabella craned her neck to see Giuliano de Medici sprawled in a pool of blood on the mosaic floor. His former supporter, Francesco Pazzi, stood over him with a bloody dagger while another man fell on him in a frenzy of violence that was terrifying.

Horrified by the nightmare that had erupted around her, Isabella dragged Caterina close to her, desperate to keep her cousin from seeing Giuliano. She glimpsed a gilded screen near the marble-inlaid wall and pushed Caterina ahead of her into its meagre shelter. The crowd trampled past them and Isabella held Caterina tight as her cousin sobbed into her shoulder.

Over Caterina's head, she watched the swirling pandemonium that turned the beautiful, soaring space into something ugly and terrifying. People were crashing into each other in their terror-filled rush to escape and the thick, metallic scent of blood drowned out the perfumes and the incense.

Isabella suddenly caught a glimpse of Matteo's bright hair. She opened her mouth to cry out to him—but the words strangled in her throat when Matteo drew his dagger and she saw who stood across from him. Orlando.

Orlando, whose handsome god's face was twisted with fury as he looked at her cousin. She barely recognized him, just as she didn't recognize the world around her. Everything seemed to move slower, in a blurred haze, and she couldn't even open her mouth to cry out. This was the moment of her worst nightmares, but it was much, much too real. And she was helpless to stop it.

Then Orlando lunged towards Matteo, his dagger raised, and Isabella finally screamed. Once she began, she could not stop.

Orlando had planned his revenge, imagined it, for so long. Matteo Strozzi was always too protected, too surrounded by his bravo friends and their swords, and Orlando wanted to have time to make sure the villain knew for what crime he paid. Wanted to look into his eyes and make sure the bastard was penitent for what he did to Maria Lorenza. For how he had left little Maria alone in the world, buried in disgrace.

Now, here in the chaos of a sudden riot in the cathedral, Orlando glimpsed his chance. Unlooked for. Matteo Strozzi was alone, his friends fled, twisting to every side as he brandished his dagger and searched frantically for a path to flee himself.

Orlando drew his own dagger and moved stealthily towards Strozzi. He didn't see the crowds who ran past him, screaming, didn't feel them jostling him or smell the blood in the air. His fury was roused and all he could think of was Maria Lorenza and his vow to her.

'Matteo Strozzi!' he shouted. The man whirled around to face him, dagger raised. A terrible smile touched Strozzi's sweat-streaked face, as if he was actually enjoying himself in the violence.

'Orlando Landucci,' he said with a strange laugh. 'Are you part of this conspiracy? Your friends can never win against the Medici...'

'Do you remember Maria Lorenza at all?' Orlando said coldly.

Something flickered behind Strozzi's eyes and his smile widened. 'The blonde whore, you mean? Why? Did I steal her from you? They say you had Lucretia, why would you want a whey-faced whelp like that girl?'

Orlando's fury froze. He had imagined this scene, planned it, for so long. But it did not feel as he thought it would. It felt evil, wrong. The man did not know his foulness and Orlando was only making himself capable of equal evil. 'You caused her death.'

Strozzi shrugged. 'Such strumpets come and go. If she was too weak to know the ways of the world, 'twas no fault of mine. You, on the other hand—you I will gladly fight. I have been waiting for this a long time.'

'She was no strumpet,' Orlando said, strangely calm. 'She was my sister.'

That finally seemed to get through to Strozzi. Family honour—that was something even a deep-dyed villain could understand. Respond to.

Strozzi lunged towards Orlando, his dagger flashing. Orlando saw in his eyes that Strozzi meant to kill. That killing gave him pleasure. His dagger was aimed right at Orlando's heart.

Orlando parried, his own blade flashing down to block the fatal advance. The two steel daggers clashed, steel scraping steel in a harsh clatter as they tangled, parted, parried again, the sound lost in the melee of the cathedral.

Strozzi was a practised swordsman and he obviously delighted in the fight, in the blood around them. Orlando managed to stay ahead of him, his own instincts on edge, his long fury for Maria Lorenza driving him, but Strozzi was a strong opponent. His attacks mounted in speed, viciousness. The tip of his blade caught Orlando's arm before he could spin away, drawing a thin line of blood.

The air of the cathedral, once so cool and

quiet, so full of the scent of incense, was thick with blood and the salty tang of steel, of panic.

Orlando pushed Strozzi away, feeling his muscles tiring in the frantic fight. Both of them drew more blood. Enough to give pain, to distract, but not to kill. The bloody marble floor under their boots turned slick, making every step perilous. Matteo slipped and fell in it, and Orlando knew his revenge had come. Every moment lasted an eternity.

And yet—yet something stayed Orlando's blade as he raised it for one last blow. A flashing memory of Isabella's smile, her dark eyes. This man was her cousin. He had done evil, but now Orlando had, as well. His soul had become as black as Strozzi's and he was disgusted with himself for it. Disgusted for bringing Isabella into the ugliness of it all.

He whirled around to try to fight his way through the panicked crowd, leaving Strozzi on the floor. He was done with it all.

'Come back and fight me!' Orlando whirled around at Strozzi's words. Strozzi gave an impatient, incoherent shout as he loomed on to his feet in the blood and raised his blade for a lunging thrust to Orlando's neck. Orlando ducked under the attack, raising his hand to deliver a counter-thrust. His dagger buried itself deep in Strozzi's side, sending his opponent crashing to the hard stone floor. Yet still Strozzi fought onwards, his attacks rougher, more frantic.

Strozzi launched himself at Orlando with a primitive shout. Orlando fell back, his dagger flashing up to meet Strozzi's in a clash that reverberated up his arm, into his whole body. His blood ran hot again as he remembered Maria Lorenza. It made him go on the attack, meeting each vicious thrust with another, harder one. Until at last his blade went deep into Strozzi's shoulder for the last time.

The dagger slid in and out again in an instant, but it was enough to send him crashing to the floor at last. And this time he did not rise again. His life's blood trickled out to mingle with the redness already on the marble. He stared up at

Orlando, his eyes full of shock and fury, until they glazed over and went sightless.

Maria Lorenza was avenged.

Orlando stared at Strozzi's body crumpled at his feet. He had his revenge, yet inside he felt only cold and hollow. Strozzi had attacked *him*; there was no remorse for a man like that. There was nothing at all. Now he was dead, just like Maria Lorenza, who had foolishly trusted in him. Just as Isabella had trusted in Orlando.

Isabella. His angel, who was surely lost to him now.

'Vivano le palle!' a shout rang out over his head. 'Rise up for the Medici! Defeat their enemies!'

Orlando saw it was Sigismondo della Stuffe, a friend of Lorenzo de Medici, exhorting for battle from the choir loft overhead. The same loft where he had once stood with Isabella and thought the world could be new and hopeful.

That was all gone now and he had to be away from the cathedral. His battle was done; he could not be caught in another.

He dropped his bloodstained dagger atop Strozzi's body and melted into the fleeing crowd. Little Maria needed him now and he knew he had to go to her.

Yet his heart was cold, numb. He could still see Isabella in his mind, her smile, her touch, and he knew she was lost to him now. If he could make amends to her…

But he had done the unthinkable. He had killed her cousin. And she was lost to him.

Chapter Twelve

'Palle! Palle! Vivano le palle!'

The shouts rang out in the hot, thick air, piercing and sharp, cresting in an ever-growing wave of hysteria. It was a tide of bloodlust, sweeping through the *calles* and *campi* of Florence like an inexorable force that had been long suppressed, long hidden behind the facade of placid stone walls and screened balconies. It had been going on for two days and would be held back no longer.

Isabella forced her way through the crowds, pushing past knots of red-faced men clutching pikes and swords, elbowing aside any who dared stand in her way. The world was hazy and tinged with grey through her black veil, but she could smell the tang of blood on the hot breeze, the thick, coppery pong of it. It blended with the usual smells of the city—the sickly sweetness of the Arno; the fruits and fish of the Mercato Vecchio, rotting in the sun; the stench of offal in the gutters, growled over by stray dogs and feral beggar children. The honeyed perfumes of the nobles, the incense that escaped in curling silver ribbons from the churches.

Today, that tinge of blood, of death, clung to everything, an inescapable cloud of doom.

'Palle! Palle!' echoed around her, the shouts soaring over the constant toll of church bells.

Isabella finally reached a small clear space, a tiny, inset doorway that was not filled with the cacophony of voices and the martial clang of steel. She ducked inside, leaning against the rough stucco wall to catch her breath. She eased aside her veil, letting the cooler, shaded air wash over her hot cheeks, easing the sting of nausea and fear. Outside her niche, the crowd surged on, bent on their murderous errands, but their roar was muffled, as if they were in some distant nightmare, unconnected with her.

A nightmare. That was what her life had become, since that horrible moment in the cathedral, when the Host was raised and all hell broke loose. The moment the Pazzi conspirators rose up to try to murder Lorenzo de Medici and his brother. Was it only yesterday? It seemed a lifetime, a century ago. And yet—it seemed it had only happened an instant ago. It kept happening, again and again, in her fevered mind. The sight of Orlando, her beautiful Orlando, and the horror he was a part of.

Was he allied with the Pazzi? Had he been lying to her all along? She no longer knew and she was lost.

She drew a handkerchief from her tight black-silk sleeve and dabbed at her aching brow. The clean scent of lemon verbena rose from the lawn folds, reviving her somewhat. She leaned back, letting the wall hold her up for a moment, fortifying herself for what she knew must come.

This house, like most of the others in Florence, was shut up tightly, shutters locked, doors barred, silent and dark. Usually, in this holy season, when the deprivations of Lent were concluded and the promise of the risen Christ celebrated, there would be feasts and banquets, dancing and music. Merriment resounding from all the four *quartieri*. Instead, there was only the blood. Blood in the sacred cathedral, bodies hung from the windows of the Signoria, dragged through the streets in a macabre parade.

Isabella pressed her handkerchief tightly to her lips, holding back a rough sob. What had become of this beautiful city, the centre of all that was civilized, all that she loved? It had vanished, all that art and learning and chivalry, swept away on a crimson tide of ancient barbarity. Barbarity Orlando had committed.

And Isabella was alone, stranded in a tiny island set at the centre of that bloody river. Matteo was dead, Caterina ill and Orlando... Orlando had wreaked this havoc on them all. She had been a great fool. An idiot to ever kiss him, dream of him. Hope for him. There was so much death…

But you are still here, her mind whispered. *You are the only one who knows the truth. The only one who can make things right.*

That thought gave her a fresh strength. Yes— she *was* the only one left. She alone could bring herself peace now and she had to press onwards. To not give in to her womanly weakness. Not now.

Isabella took in one more deep breath of the damp, clean air, and reached up to readjust the folds of her veil. Her fingers were streaked with pinkish paint, the nails crusted at their base with a darker burgundy. The paint *would* stay, no matter how much she scrubbed, how much of Caterina's scented cream she rubbed into the skin. For an instant, it was as if she glimpsed the future—her hands stained with yet more blood.

She shoved the ghastly thought away. There was no time for such fancies now. Carefully, she leaned out of the doorway, peering both ways down the narrow *calle*.

The crowd was thinner now. Most of them had moved on, either to the courtyard of the Signoria to further defile the hanging corpses of the Pazzi, or to the traitors' *palazzi* to join in the wild orgy of ransacking. She could still hear the shouts, though—*'Vivano le palle!'*

She stepped out of her tiny haven and hurried on her way, lifting the hem of her black skirts from the damp, slick cobblestones. She wore stout boots today, her fashionable velvet slippers left at home, along with all her cowering servants. This was a journey she had to make alone.

It was a journey that usually took only minutes, a pleasant stroll from her cousins' house to the church of San Lorenzo. But not today. Today, the voyage had taken almost an hour and at the end of it there would be no sanctuary.

Isabella at last reached the church. There was another crowd gathered there, of course, but they were quieter than the roving mobs, sombre, grey-faced. The great bells of San Lorenzo tolled slowly, ponderously, drowning out the mutters and muffled curses. The clusters of black-clad men parted to let Isabella through, not jostling her or snatching at her veil as the others had. She hurried up the stone steps to the marble facade, her throat tight and painful.

At the closed wooden doors stood two soldiers, clad in the livery of the Medici. Their crossed pikes barred the way to any who dared seek entrance to the sacred space.

'Forgive us, *madonna*,' one of the stern-faced guards said. She remembered him from the party on the Prato, a friend of Giuliano's. 'Our orders are that none are to have admittance this day.'

Isabella swept aside her veil, revealing her face. 'None, *signor*? Even a Strozzi?'

'Signorina Spinola,' the guard said, his voice tinged with surprise. 'I do not know...'

'Please, *signor*. I want only to see him before they carry him to the vault. I will cause no trouble. Surely Signor Lorenzo would give me that chance?'

The two soldiers exchanged quick glances, finally drawing back their pikes after a long, heavy moment. 'Of course, *madonna*.'

'*Grazie*.' Isabella edged through the small space between their pikes. As she pushed open one of the heavy doors, they crossed again behind her, a metallic clash barring all who would dare disturb the peace of the church.

Isabella blinked at the sudden gloom, after the heavy heat of the day. She let her veil rest on her shoulders, baring her gaze to the dark, soaring space. A few candles flickered along the aisles, casting a pale, golden glow over the stone floors, the serene faces of the saints. The air was chilly, faintly touched with the sweetness of incense, the beeswax of the rich candles. And, underneath, something deeper. Darker.

The smell of death. Of decay. Of unending grief.

A single sob rose up, seemingly from nowhere, rising to the high patterns of the ceiling and hanging there, a single note of perfect despair, before dissipating like the incense smoke. Isabella shivered, that cry echoing inside of her, a mirror of her own fresh sorrow. For an instant, she longed to turn away, to run back down those violent streets to the safety of her own house. To hide away from all of this.

But she knew she could not. It would chase her wherever she went, for ever. She could only go forward, slowly, painfully, one foot at a time. Orlando would always be there, haunting her.

As he did now, in the church where once they had kissed. She walked carefully down the centre aisle, her footsteps echoing dully, an intrusion in that perfect silence. Before the high altar lay the body of Giuliano de Medici, surrounded by a ring of silently praying, black-cowled monks. Twenty-five years old, the 'radiant sun' of the Medici, cut down. And Caterina grief-stricken.

Isabella crossed herself before his velvet-draped bier. His wounds were concealed beneath a rich, fur-edged robe, by the edges of the opaque shroud that waited to enclose him. His handsome face, framed by the tumble of his dark, glossy hair, was unmarked and he lay in pale peacefulness, a martyred saint. Though he hadn't been the least bit saint-like in life.

Isabella turned towards one of the side chapels, the Sagrestia Nuova. Here, there were two biers, less grand than Giuliano's, but still draped in velvets, surrounded by the glow of candles. Francesco Nori, Lorenzo de Medici's great friend, lay on one.

The other bier, set deeper in the shadows, bore Matteo.

Isabella's steps slowed and stilled as she peered deeper into the dim shadows of the chapel, her stomach tightening into a sour knot. Another wave of nausea rose up in her throat and she swallowed hard against the bitterness. She could not be sick, not now. She could not give in to her crazed emotions, the wild urge to scream, to sob, to tear at her hair. *Not now.*

Oh, Blessed Mother, she prayed. *Help me now!*

Clinging to that thought of the Virgin watching over her, guiding her with cool, blue serenity, Isabella narrowed her eyes and peered closer.

She bit her lip to hold back a sudden cry as she at last looked down at Matteo's familiar face and the truth struck her as never before. Not even when she saw him fall in the cathedral, saw that dagger plunge into his chest, had she *known* as she knew now. Her cousin was dead and Orlando had killed him.

Slowly, Isabella sank to her knees on the floor beside the chapel entrance. She barely felt the hard chill of the marble beneath her legs, barely heard anything above the buzzing in her head, like a flock of demented bees.

She clasped her hands tightly in prayer. 'Remember me, Matteo, wherever you are,' she whispered. 'And rest in peace, knowing that you will not go unavenged.'

She herself would avenge him, as family honour demanded. Even though to do so would destroy her own heart, a heart she had never known she possessed until she met *him*. Orlando. The man she had dared to dream of, to imagine might be her love.

But why, why had he done that? He had never seemed to have any family alliances among the Pazzi. In fact, she remembered the look of faint derision he tossed them at the riverside party. Why, why? The question plagued her, would never let her alone. She needed answers.

'Orlando,' she whispered, her whole body aching as if she would break. She had come to Florence so full of ridiculous hopes, so sure that here, amid the art and beauty of this city, she would find herself. But she had only lost everything. Her art. Her heart. Her soul, if she did now what she knew she had to do.

Isabella could have wept, wailed. *Too late, too late.* Any fire she had ever possessed, any passion, was gone. She folded her hands tightly at her waist to still their shaking, to hold back the hot, salty flood of tears. She had no time to cry now. The time for tears, like the time for love, was long past.

* * *

Orlando drew in his horse at the crest of the tallest hill outside Florence and glanced back at the city, even though he knew he should not. The domes and towers of the city rose into the dusky sky, golden and rosy, like a distant dream. He felt such a deep compulsion to grab that image, that last impression of his home to take with him in his memory, even though he knew time was slipping away from him. If he was found, he would surely die. He had to find a haven.

But there, in the Florence he was leaving behind, was her. Isabella.

Night was falling fast, a blanket of purplish light drifting down that slowly concealed the town. From here, all looked quiet, serene. But there were orange-red flickers from the bonfires lit to celebrate the demise of the Pazzi conspirators, the revenge of the Medici on the family who would have destroyed them.

The flames suddenly shot up likes beacons in the blackness, sparks of brilliant red and rosy-gold, exploding, bringing to mind horrible images of burning bodies.

Orlando rubbed his hand over his unshaven jaw. He'd waited so very long to take his own revenge, had planned for it, craved it. Matteo Strozzi deserved his death and innocents were safer with him gone from the world. And yet…

Yet when the moment of his revenge came, it wasn't at all what he had so long envisioned. It did not erase the wrongs of the past. It only increased them a hundredfold.

An explosion shot over the tiled rooftops of the city, a burst of sparkling light and noise. Where was Isabella now? Locked in her family's house, mourning, in fear? Afraid of *him*?

Or was her secret heart even now filling with the hate that infected the whole city?

Orlando thought of Isabella as he had first seen her, in Signor Botticelli's studio. Her shining eyes as she gazed at the art around her, the bright openness of her smile. The smile she gave *him*, as if they shared a rare, wonderful secret. If he had robbed her of that smile…

'*Maledizione,*' he cursed. He'd *had* to confront Matteo Strozzi there in the chaos of the cathedral. His family's honour, the memory of Maria Lorenza, demanded it and he was not a man to turn away from his duty, no matter that his family thought him only a wastrel.

But his heart now felt—blackened. Twisted out of human recognition when he remembered Isabella and the few, fleeting, precious moments they shared.

Isabella. He would return for her. He would make her see the truth. If it was the very last thing he could ever do.

Chapter Thirteen

'In a short time passes every great rain; and the warmth makes disappear the snows and ice that make the rivers look so proud...'

Caterina's bedchamber was dark and shadowy, the shutters drawn against the brightness of the day, the air stuffy and filled with the heavy scents of undrunk wine and uneaten food. Caterina lay still under the embroidered counterpane of her bed, her eyes staring unseeing at the canopy above her. She didn't seem to hear Isabella reading, or the servants tiptoeing around, yet still Isabella read on from her chair by the bed.

She didn't know what else to do. Whenever she ceased speaking, her thoughts washed over her again. Terrible, terrible images of blood and screams. That dagger in Orlando's hand. Matteo dead on the cathedral floor.

Nay, if she thought of it she feared she would start screaming and would never cease. So she read on, until her voice was hoarse and she could barely see straight.

At last, as the sun began to turn golden-rosy at the edges of the windows, Caterina stirred. She rolled on to her side, her tangled golden hair weaving around her like a drowning mermaid.

'No love poetry, Isabella, I beg you,' she whispered.

'You are awake!' Isabella cried in relief. She had so feared to lose both her cousins in these long, lonely hours. She tossed aside the book and reached for Caterina's hand. It was pale and ice-cold. 'We have been so very worried. Let me call the doctor back…'

'Nay, no more doctors,' Caterina said. She curled her fingers around Isabella's, her grasp surprisingly strong. Desperate. 'They cannot help me now.'

'But you haven't stirred in days,' Isabella argued. 'At least take a little wine.'

Caterina nodded and let Isabella help her sip from the goblet. When she was done, she fell back to the pillows, her face as white as the linens. Over her laboured breath, they could hear the shouts that still rang out from the streets below. The toll of the church bells. The death still went on.

But Isabella could not think of that now. Could not think of how they were trapped in this house, how beautiful, elegant Florence had become a battleground in only a moment. She had to think of Caterina. Caterina had lost her brother and her suitor Giuliano.

And Isabella had dared to cherish tender feelings for the very man who had killed Matteo. It froze her to think of it now, to know how blind and dangerously foolish she had been. How could she not have seen the truth of it in his eyes? Feel it in his kiss?

Yet all she had seen was his beauty. All she had felt was her own happiness when he held her in his arms.

Now she paid the price for that foolishness.

She tucked the bedclothes around Caterina. 'What can I bring you, Caterina? If you will not see the doctor…'

'He can do nothing for me,' Caterina said. She closed her eyes again. 'We cannot stay here, Isabella. We must leave Florence as soon as the streets are safe.'

Isabella nodded. She, too, wanted to see the last of this city. Its art and beauty had turned to ashes in her mouth. 'Where shall we go?'

'You must return to your father. I was selfish to ever take you from him. And I will go to the convent of St Ursula, in the hills. I have a friend who is abbess there. She will make a place for me. Perhaps I can find rest there one day.' A spasm of pain crossed Caterina's face.

'Shall I not go there with you?'

Caterina shook her head. Her hand tightened on Isabella's. 'You can go with me to make sure all is well, but then I must beg you to do something for me before you go home.'

'Of course,' Isabella said. 'I will do anything I can to help you, Cousin.'

'I am too weak to do the proper duty to my brother,' Caterina whispered. 'So I must beg you to do it for me, for our family honour.'

Family honour? Was that not what had begun this whole nightmare in the first place? Yet Isabella could not refuse her cousin, who looked so ill, so grief-stricken. She had to do her duty now, as she had so neglected it in her own romantic dream. 'What is it?'

'You must find out who did this to Matteo and see that he pays his blood debt.'

Isabella froze. How could she possibly tell Caterina she knew who did it?

Yet how could she refuse her? As Caterina said, this was their family. Orlando had to pay for what he had done, according to the code of their world. No matter why he did it, what his thoughts were now.

'I—I will try,' she told Caterina.

Caterina nodded and turned her head away. 'I wish to see Matteo once more, before he is buried.'

'You are too tired,' Isabella said. 'Just sleep now. Tomorrow we will leave for St Ursula's, if you are strong enough.'

Caterina could only squeeze Isabella's hand weakly one more time. The herbs mixed in the wine were doing their task and soon she would be asleep.

But as Isabella turned away to draw off her black veil, she feared she herself would not sleep again for a very long while.

'You must leave Florence.'

Orlando stared out of the window of Botticelli's studio, barely hearing the artist's words. He saw a group of boys parade past, a head on a pike, as gleeful as at a holy day parade. The whole city had descended into just such carnage after the cathedral. And he had been a part of it. Helped tear apart the fabric of the beautiful city with his own hands.

Yet he felt so removed. So numb. All he could think of was what he was leaving behind. What he had lost before he barely even found it.

Isabella. His one moment of transcendence. She was gone from him. He had gained his long-sought revenge. Maria Lorenza could rest at last. Yet it was hollow and cold.

'Aye, I must go,' he said. He glanced back at his friend.

Botticelli nodded, calmly cleaning his brushes as if the carnage outside his window didn't exist. 'Yet there is no hue and cry for your death. No riders out hunting for you.'

'What I did had nothing to do with Pazzis and Medici.'

'Nay. You did what you thought you had to do. Now you can go on with your life.'

Orlando gave a bitter laugh. His life for so long had been about revenge. Now—there was nothing there. He had only glimpsed the life he might have had, the dream of it, for a few moments with Isabella.

'I can do that away from Florence,' he said.

Botticelli looked doubtful. 'Where will you go?'

'To my kinsman, the lord of the town of Fiencosole, at first. There is something important I must do there. Then I will seek a place in a foreign army. My sword arm must be worth something.' After he saw little Maria safe, he had nothing else left to lose.

'A mercenary?'

'Aye, why not?'

'Why not indeed?' Botticelli said musingly. He laid aside his brushes. 'I will help you in any way I can, my friend. If you are determined to toss away your life, then you must do it. But remember—fate always has a way of surprising us.'

Orlando laughed. Fate had not been his friend thus far. He imagined that wouldn't change. 'I hope fate may at least leave me alone now. I have had quite enough of her whims.'

Botticelli just smiled. 'Oh, no, Orlando. You will see...'

Chapter Fourteen

Isabella stared up at the painting on Botticelli's studio wall. Springtime—the same glorious, beautiful rebirth that held her entranced the first day she came there with Caterina. The goddess in her flower-strewn gown, her acolytes dancing around her in the warmth of the dappled sunlight. Once it had made her feel as if all things were possible, as if life was opening up before her in all its infinite possibilities.

Now when she looked at it she felt only numb. Cold.

The studio was echoingly silent, empty. All the apprentices were gone, their work scattered over the tables and easels. Only the servant who let her in, the one who promised to go find Botticelli for her, was a sign of life.

From beyond the windows, Isabella could still hear the shouts of *'Palle! Palle!'* that had followed her when she left Matteo's bier at the cathedral. There were crashes, the diamond-sharp rattle of broken glass, screams. But in the studio everything was eerily still.

Isabella stared up at the face of the goddess, her serenity, her small, secret smile. Once she had worn just such a smile, thinking of Orlando. Of how he made her feel.

You are my family now, Caterina had sobbed. And family avenged each other.

'Signorina Isabella,' Botticelli said behind her. 'I did not think to see anyone today.'

'I went to the cathedral to see Matteo earlier,' Isabella said shortly.

'Of course.' Botticelli came to her side and studied her carefully, his handsome face expressionless. 'And how does Signorina Caterina today?'

'She keeps to her bed. She says she will retreat to a convent soon.'

'Perhaps the peace of a cloister would help her find rest,' Botticelli said. 'Giuliano cared for her more than she would acknowledge, I fear. She thought him only a rogue, but he thought she was—different. Above everyone else.'

As Isabella had once thought Orlando? She cringed now to remember the naive joy his kiss had awakened in her. What a fool she had been! She had thought him different, as well, but he was only a part of the violent ugliness Florence hid beneath the marble towers and bright frescoes.

He was truly the god of the Underworld, but not in the brooding, romantically longing way she had imagined. He was the god of bloodshed and death.

Isabella bit her lip to hold back a scream as she remembered that flashing dagger in his hand, the blood splashed lurid red on the pale marble floor. It was an image that would surely haunt her every time she dared close her eyes.

Her heart felt heavy and hard in her chest, as if she, too, had turned to stone.

'Signor Botticelli,' she said. 'You know a man called Orlando. I have seen him here at your studio.'

His expression did not change, but she thought she saw something flicker in his eyes. He crossed his arms across his broad chest. 'You look for him?'

'I am sure he has fled Florence by now,' she said. 'After what happened in the cathedral…'

'And what happened there, Signorina Isabella?'

Isabella felt a surge of anger. 'He killed my cousin in the riot. I saw him.'

Botticelli shook his head and Isabella was surprised to see that he looked suddenly sad. 'Are you certain of what you saw? There was much confusion there. So many people certain that marauders had desecrated our fair city.'

'I know what I saw,' she said through gritted teeth. 'Matteo was my family.'

'Of course he was and his sister is my friend.

Yet think, *signorina*—what did you truly know of Matteo Strozzi? Of his past deeds, his character? You are an artist, a sensitive soul. You can see deeper than most.'

'I know what I saw!' Isabella cried. 'What do you mean about my cousin's past deeds? What can they have been to cause his murder?'

Botticelli opened his mouth as if to say something, but then he closed it and shook his head again. His broad forehead creased in a frown. ''Tis not my tale to tell, I fear. Just remember what I said. Trust only your own instincts. Do nothing in the heat of temper. That is what leads so many here in Florence into sin and trouble.'

Isabella looked up at the painting once more. She saw hope there again and she feared she would never feel that again. 'Do you know where Orlando is?' she said. That was why she had come to the studio from the cathedral. Botticelli was Orlando's friend and as an artist he had contacts in many places. He would know things others would not.

Botticelli was silent for a long moment. 'Perhaps, like your cousin Caterina, you would care for a time of reflection.'

Isabella gave a harsh laugh. 'I have not the spirit for a convent.'

'Nay, not you. But there are many kinds of reflection. I have always found painting to be the best.' He went to a table in the corner, heaped with parchments and half-finished sketches, and reached for a quill pen and pot of ink. 'I have a friend who works for the lord of a town called Fiencosole. He was once an apprentice of mine. He has a fine way with the drape of cloth in a painting. He would be happy to instruct you.'

'Fiencosole?' Isabella said, confused. She did know of the place, it was not far from her father's home and had a beautiful fresco cycle in its old cathedral. But she had never been there.

He shrugged. ''Tis not a grand place like Florence, but the lord is an artistic and learned man. His court is one of great refinement. You would like it there.'

'I have no time for art now,' she argued.

'There is always time for art.' He came to her and held out the hastily written missive, which she saw was a letter of introduction. 'And I am sure you will find what you seek in Fiencosole, Isabella, if you will only look for it.'

Isabella studied his face carefully, hoping to read his true meaning there, but it was blank. Finally she nodded and took the letter from his hand. 'Very well,' she said. 'I will go there, and see what I find.'

'She is doing very well today, *signor*,' the abbess of the convent of St Clare said as she led Orlando down the stone corridor, towards the light of the gardens.

'No more nightmares?' Orlando said. His booted footsteps sounded loud on the flagstone floor. He always felt like a large, hard intruder in the hush of the cloister, where only whispers and the rustle of woollen habits broke the sacred, flower-scented silence. But little Maria needed him.

'None at all,' the abbess said. 'She will be happy to see you. She asks after you so often.'

'I am sorry I have been kept away too long,' he answered.

'You take such good care of her, *signor*.'

At the arched doorway to the garden, Orlando paused to watch the lovely scene in front of him. Maria dashed through the bright green and tumbled white flowers of the herbal plots, laughing as two sisters playfully chased her in their black-and-white habits. Her childish giggles floated to him, lighter than the sunlit air.

Her laughter seemed to wash over him, carrying away some of the blood and ugliness that had marred his soul since the violence in the cathedral. He had done the greatest sin in a sacred place, all for his vow to avenge the wrongs of the past. Yet the past seemed closer than ever. Matteo Strozzi was gone, but his deeds remained. Now Orlando had added to the terror of it all.

He thought again of Isabella, his beautiful angel, his saint, the woman whose innocence gave him back a part of his blackened soul—only for him to lose it again. The priests were right. Evil only begat evil, in perpetuity, and he hadn't ended it when he fought with Strozzi.

He looked up to meet the blank eyes of a marble Madonna. Her sad calm, her offered hand, reminded him of Isabella. He wished he could take her hand, let her save him, but that was gone now.

'Uncle Orlando!' Maria cried in her sweet, high child's voice. 'You're here at last.'

He turned just in time to catch her in his arms as she threw herself at him. She was so small, light as swansdown in his embrace, but she healed him just a bit with her smile. He had avenged her and her mother at last, just as he had vowed to do.

Why then did he feel so very empty?

Maria wound her little arms around his neck. 'Will you stay here this time, Uncle Orlando? At least until the summer?'

Orlando laughed wryly as he kissed her cheek. 'I will stay here, Maria.' He could not go back to Florence, not now. He had to make a new life, for himself and Maria. They were all they had now, each other.

A life where he would never see Isabella again. And somehow he knew the black chill in his heart, the chill Isabella had warmed all too briefly, would never leave him again.

Chapter Fifteen

'Any pupil of Botticelli is certainly most welcome at Fiencosole!' Signor Salle, Botticelli's protégé and now court artist to the lord of the town of Fiencosole, led Isabella down a long corridor lined with half-finished frescoes. A few apprentices scurried up and down ladders, bearing palettes and baskets. 'As you can see, there is much work to be done. His lordship wishes to cover the whole *palazzo* with art.'

Isabella tilted back her head to examine a scene of a banquet. Classical gods in diaphanous draperies gathered around a table laden with glistening fruit and spilled ewers of wine, while fat little cupids flitted around their laurel-crowned heads. It was a bright scene, full of laughter.

Hades would never fit in there. Nor would she, in her new black gown and veil.

'I fear I am no pupil of Botticelli, *signor*,' she said. 'Merely an amateur. I was most fortunate he befriended me. But I am happy to help you in any way I can. I can mix plaster, grind colours…'

Signor Salle laughed. 'He says you can do much more than that! But forgive me. He also writes that you need rest and clean country air after a sad loss. I see you are in mourning.'

'Thank you. My cousin was killed in the— troubles in Florence. I am very grateful for your hospitality. Work will be very beneficial, I think.'

Work—and taking her revenge, as a Strozzi should. She just had no idea how to get close to Orlando now that she was here in Fiencosole, or even if he did indeed reside there. She had no experience at this revenge business and little stomach for it. But there was no one else to do it.

She wandered to an open window and stared down at the courtyard below. The lord of Fiencosole walked there, a tall man with long, greying dark hair straggling from beneath his cap and a velvet robe draped around his spare figure. Crowds of people and dogs trailed after him. A small city Fiencosole might be, but it had more than its share of courtiers and petitioners, swelled by the ranks of those fleeing Florence.

Her task would not be easy.

Signor Salle peered over her shoulder. 'Ah, his lordship has returned from the hunt. He will want to meet you.'

'Should I not change my garb?' she asked, studying the fine embroidered silks of the ladies.

'You are in mourning, *signorina*. Everyone will understand. And he will want to hear the latest news from Florence.'

The latest news from Florence. The last Isabella had seen, glimpsed from behind the curtains of Caterina's carriage as they left the city, were bodies dangling from windows of the Pazzi house. Blood on cobblestones. She had to turn away before she could be sick.

Now Caterina was safe in her convent, thinking Isabella on her way to her father's villa. And so she would be, once she accomplished her grim duty.

Or perhaps she would have to enter a convent herself and spend the rest of her life doing penance for her sins.

She remembered Orlando again, his smile in the moonlight, his quiet beauty as he studied the cathedral from their loft. Why, oh, why could he have not been what he appeared? Why did he have to cast her into this nightmare?

'Thank you, Signor Salle,' she said, turning away from the window. 'You have been most kind.'

He led her down the stone steps at the end of the corridor and into the garden where the courtiers were clustered. Their laughter sounded foreign after the bloody visions of Florence, the smells of the flowers and their perfumes thick and strange.

Isabella scanned every face, but Orlando's was not among them. She would have to find time to examine every inch of the town, whose spires and rooftops could be glimpsed over the ivy-covered garden wall. He could not hide for ever, she knew every detail of his face and form all too well.

The man she had thought he was, the man who had kissed her on the terrace, would not hide. But then, she realized with a sharp pang, that man had never actually existed.

'Signorina Spinola! We welcome you to Fiencosole,' the lord said as she curtsied before him. 'We are eager to hear of the newest art in Florence…'

As he asked her more questions, Isabella suddenly had a prickling, icy feeling at the back of her neck. As discreetly as possible, she glanced behind her, shielding her face with edge of her black veil.

Orlando stood there in the gateway to the courtyard.

At first, she was frozen with the shock of actually seeing him there. The warm day felt suddenly icy and she didn't know what to do. Where to hide.

But he didn't notice her there. From the concealment of her veil, Isabella studied him carefully. He wore dark garments, as he always did, and his glossy black hair was tousled by the breeze. When he impatiently pushed it back, she saw his classically handsome face was marred by a new, ugly red scar. The wages of the evil that happened in the cathedral?

And yet he was smiling. *Smiling.* Isabella couldn't believe he dared to do so. Then she saw what he smiled down on—a little girl who held on to his hand.

Isabella's heart seemed to squeeze in her chest and she couldn't breathe. The girl looked like a tiny angel in a pale blue gown and hooded cloak, her red-gold curls tumbling around her shoulders. She held tight to Orlando's hand, bouncing in excitement, and it was obvious they were close.

Was she—could she be his daughter?

Isabella pressed her hand to her mouth to keep from crying out. If he had a child, how could she do what she promised Matteo she would? How could she bear to? Yet how could she forget her vow?

Her stern resolve wavering, she turned sharply away from the sight.

'I hope you will attend our masked ball to-morrow night, *signorina*,' his lordship said suddenly, jerking her attention from Orlando and the child, and her own confused thoughts. 'I know you are in mourning, but I have some of the finest musicians to be found outside of Florence. Music can lift the spirits, just as great paintings can, I always say.'

A ball? Where she could hide behind a mask and find out more about her quarry? 'I would be honoured to attend,' Isabella murmured.

'Excellent!' he said, clapping his hands. 'And perhaps you can inspect my artworks in progress, and tell me how they compare to Signor Botticelli's work...'

He and his courtiers continued on their path through the garden. And when Isabella glanced back, Orlando and the little girl had disappeared.

Chapter Sixteen

Isabella could hear music as she made her way down the curving marble staircase and along the winding halls of the *palazzo*, a merry *passamiento* that seemed to mock her dark, confused thoughts. She kept seeing Orlando, his smile at the little girl. And Orlando, standing over her cousin's body at the cathedral. Which was the real man?

She paused next to a silver-framed Venetian looking glass to adjust her mask. She almost didn't recognize herself in her new costume, a classically draped gown of diaphanous apricot and cream, caught at the shoulders with golden brooches like an Aphrodite or Artemis. Her hair was covered by an elaborately curled blond wig, bound by a gold wreath of laurel leaves. Her features were concealed by a gold satin half-mask, her lips tinted red.

If she did not even recognize herself, then surely Orlando would not either. If he was even there at all…

Her stomach clenched and she feared she would be sick.

Give me strength, she silently begged. Strength to do what she had to do. What was right.

And yet—what *was* right? The sight of the little girl had changed so much, had made her doubt. Surely she would know what to do when she was face to face with Orlando.

Isabella turned in a flurry of skirts and rushed towards the noise of the music, which flooded out through the open doors of the grand salon. Small the city of Fiencosole might be, but its lord lived well in his court. Turkish carpets were laid over the cold stone floors and intricately carved cameos looked down from roundels high on the mottled stone walls, watching the party.

She stepped through the salon doors and into a summer wonderland. Botticelli's painting come to life. Garlands of dark green ivy and pale flowers twined around the thick marble pillars and damask-draped tables held gold and silver platters of pasta, roasted chickens and pheasants, fish garlanded with lemons, towering white cakes of beaten eggs and sugar. Pages in miniature silver chitons scurried past, keeping goblets filled with ruby-red wine.

Isabella examined the musicians who played with great gusto in their gallery above the crowd. The dancers twirled and spun past in an intricate pattern, their classical robes pale against the greenery as their arms linked and broke apart again. She watched each face carefully, trying to see past the masks. How very deeply she wanted to find Orlando—and yet how she dreaded it, too.

She took a goblet of wine from one of the pages and sipped at its sweetness as she made her way around the edge of the dancers. She studied every face, every manly figure, yet none of them was Orlando.

'*Signora!*' A tall, obviously ale-shot Adonis suddenly grabbed her arm and twirled her around. 'Dance with me, my goddess!'

Isabella laughed. She was certainly in no dancing mood, but if there was one thing she had learned in Florence it was how to hide her emotions. 'I cannot dance tonight, *signor.*'

'Everyone must dance on such a night as this.' He twirled her around as Isabella tried to slide out of his arms and everything around her turned blurry.

As she spun, she suddenly caught a glimpse of darkness amid the brilliant colours of the dance. She pushed the Adonis away and swung around frantically to see what it was.

Orlando stood in the doorway. He wore a mask like everyone else and his dark hair was brushed severely back, but she was sure it was him. No one else had strong shoulders like that. He turned and left before even joining the dance and Isabella ran after him, frantic.

At first he was lost in the knots of people who milled around the corridor, partaking of the delicacies and flirting together. Isabella glanced one way, then the other, trying to move around the courtiers without elbowing them aside and causing a scene. Finally she glimpsed him turning through a doorway and ran after him.

She slid around the corner to see him making his way down a narrower, tapestry-lined hallway, where the merriment of the party was muffled. He moved quickly, as confidently as ever, yet she sensed something more—careful about his steps.

'*Signor!*' she called.

His shoulders stiffened and his hand flew to the hilt of the dagger at his waist. He spun around in one graceful movement, like a cat, to face her. She could see nothing of his expression behind the mask, but she thought he went very still with surprise. At least he didn't leave.

Yet now that she faced him again at last, she didn't quite know what to do. She tried to remember Caterina, the way she had smiled at

Giuliano, the way she swayed towards him and glanced up at him from beneath her lashes. That was how to be alluring.

Isabella drew in a deep breath and made herself smile. She walked slowly towards him, hoping her gown flowed enticingly. Hoping he didn't leave again and make her chase him down.

He watched her move closer, his hand still on his dagger.

'Leaving before you even have a dance?' she whispered, keeping her voice low and rough. She slumped so she seemed shorter and hoped her wig and face paint was enough in the dim light. She had learned how to behave like another person entirely. It had to be enough.

He gave her a strange, small smile. 'I fear I am not in a dancing mood, *signora*,' he said, politely.

'You cannot be persuaded at all?' she asked. She reached out to gently touch his velvet sleeve—and then she realized her great mistake.

This was not merely some monster of her

imagining, the villain of the chaos in the cathedral. This was *Orlando*, the man who had kissed her, who she dared dream about. Her poetic hero, who climbed balconies for her. He hadn't changed so much since he held her on the terrace. He smelled the same, felt the same.

Had the same effect on her.

Nay! she thought sternly. She pushed away the rush of feelings and made herself remember instead the blood and panic of the cathedral.

He laughed roughly. 'I came to the ball as a favour to my kinsman.'

'Your kinsman?'

'The lord of this house.'

Ah, so that was why he came to Fiencosole, to shelter with his kinsman from Florentine wrath. But who was the little girl? And why had he killed Matteo at all?

'But I fear I must retire now,' he said. He took her hand and raised it to his lips for a quick salute. It was light, impersonal, not at all like the way he once touched her, yet it still made her shiver. 'Thank you for your kind invitation.'

Isabella couldn't let him leave. Not until she had more answers. She held on to his arm. 'It is too lovely a night to be alone, when there is such music and wine to be had...'

Suddenly, a loud, drunken group tumbled through the doorway into their private corridor. Isabella impulsively grabbed Orlando's hand and pulled him with her behind the shelter of a tapestry.

'*Signora...*' he said, laughing.

Isabella was desperate to keep him from leaving. 'It's too beautiful a night to be alone with one's thoughts, isn't it?' She pressed him to the stone wall, her hands against his shoulders. Beneath the fine satin of his doublet, he felt so hard, so strong. Yet he didn't push her away.

His eyes darkened behind his mask. 'Who are you?'

'No one of importance,' she answered. 'Just someone trying to lose myself behind these masks, *signor*. I think you would understand that.'

His whole body grew taut under her touch. '*Signora*, I don't comprehend you.'

Isabella stared up at him. In his eyes she saw none of the darkness she expected, only curiosity. Wariness. Not knowing what else to do, she went up on tiptoe and kissed him.

At first it was only desperation to keep him with her that drove her, but as soon as her lips touched his, as soon as she tasted him, she remembered the intoxication of his embrace. The fire that always caught between them. His arms closed around her and drew her closer, and she gasped as she felt the touch of his tongue on hers. It was wondrous, perfect, as if she had suddenly come back to where she belonged.

It was horrible, because she knew what she had to do. Yet she couldn't quite let go of him, not yet.

So he did it for her.

'*Signora!*' Orlando pushed her away. His hands on her arms were gentle but very firm, not letting her closer, but not making her go away either. 'I know not what game you play.

You are most interesting, but I fear my heart is far away from here tonight.'

His heart was far away? Could he mean… was it…?

She let him go, her hands suddenly too numb to hold on to him. He bowed and left her there behind the tapestry. She listened to his footsteps grow fainter on the marble floor and leaned her forehead against the cold wall. She closed her eyes and tried to make her whirling thoughts stop.

Yet now she had even more questions than before and no answers at all.

She took a deep breath and left her sheltered spot. A page was hurrying past, a ewer of wine in his hands.

'Excuse me,' she called. 'Which chamber belongs to that man in the black doublet…?'

Orlando tossed his discarded doublet atop the clothes' chest at the foot of his borrowed bed and reached for the goblet of wine left on the table. He finished it in one long swallow, but the rich brew could not banish the strange mood of the night. The memory of the masked woman's eyes, so endlessly dark, deep as the night outside. Something about them haunted him.

He poured himself more wine and went to peer out the window. The hour grew late and the party had spilled out into the garden. Lanterns hung from the trees, casting an amber glow over the costumed figures dancing over the grass. They looked like the ancient, frozen scenes on Grecian urns.

Their laughter drifted up to him, yet it could not touch him, couldn't penetrate the armour he had built again around his heart. Isabella had torn it down with her dainty, paint-stained fingers, with her smile and the innocent glow of her eyes. For one brief moment, he had glimpsed sunlight again, hope.

That was ripped apart that terrible day in the cathedral. He had his revenge—but he had lost his heart. Now he had to take care of his niece, secure her future. It was for Maria alone that he kept moving forward.

He stared down at the dancers and found himself wondering if one of them was the masked woman who had kissed him so suddenly. Yet there was none with that colour of gown. She seemed to have vanished as suddenly as she appeared, which was fortunate. He had no time or inclination for the arts of Eros now.

Yet there had been something in her eyes as he drew away from her, something that tugged at his memory and his senses now. Could it be possible…?

Orlando frowned as he swallowed the last of the wine and tossed aside the goblet. The liquor flowed through his veins, bringing a measure of warm forgetfulness at last. It mattered not who the woman was, or what she wanted from him. His heart was gone now, leaving him hollow.

He shed his shirt and fell across the waiting bed. He could only pray his dreams would cease to haunt him for this one night…

Chapter Seventeen

The *palazzo* was silent as Isabella tiptoed out of her chamber. Almost eerily so, as if the night had closed its dark tentacles around them all and put them under a sleeping spell. The salon was deserted, shadowed, scattered with empty goblets, wilted flowers, and greyhounds fighting over the remains of the feast.

Isabella shivered. Surely there was nothing sadder than the remains of a party when everyone had left. All of Florence had felt like that when she took Caterina away. Would Fiencosole become just such another place now?

Her stomach tightened painfully as she remembered the blood and terror of Florence. Her life had always been about art, about making the world more beautiful and more orderly. Now she had set out to take all of that apart, just as the Pazzi had.

Isabella glanced over her shoulder back to the darkened staircase. She didn't feel like herself that night. It was as if she hovered somewhere high above, watching as she moved through the deserted halls. She didn't know herself any longer, didn't know the world around her.

But she had set her course when she held Caterina's hand and promised her she would take care of things. She had to finish it. She had to discover the truth, about Orlando and Matteo. About herself.

She closed her eyes for an instant, remembering the look on Orlando's face when he turned away from her behind the tapestry. Had she gone mad, or did he, could he, miss her? Regret what happened? Mayhap all her feelings in Florence had not been mere imaginings. Mere fancies.

But why, then, had he done what he did at the cathedral?

Isabella stiffened her shoulders and her resolve. She would discover it all tonight. She drew the hood of her cloak closer around her face and hurried onwards.

The corridor where the page told her Orlando's chamber lay was as silent as the rest of the *palazzo*. Torches in their sconces flickered, lighting the way. The rich tapestries on the walls muffled any sound at all, except for a quickly cut-off gasp and cry from behind one of the doors. But it was not from Orlando's chamber.

His room was at the very end of the corridor. Isabella's stomach still hurt and she could hardly breathe. For an instant, she longed to flee, to forget all of this had ever happened, but it was far too late for that now.

She reached out and gently pushed the door open.

The window was half-open, letting in stray silvery beams of moonlight that fell across the polished floor. It was a small space, but grand, with carved furniture, a painting of a serene, blue-draped Madonna on the panelled wall and a damask curtain at the window.

Isabella turned away from the Madonna's sad smile and found the large bed set up on a dais. One candle was lit on the table beside it, casting shadows on the green curtains.

A tangle of dark garments lay atop a clothes' chest at the foot of the bed and the embroidered curtains were half-drawn back. In the moonlight, she could glimpse a pale, rumpled sheet and one hand flung out. The long, elegant fingers she remembered all too well were curled into a fist, as if he fought even in his dreams.

Her feelings were so confused in her. She longed for him and hated him all at the same time.

She forced herself to breathe, pushing away her fear and gathering an icy-cold mantel around herself. She drew out the dagger she had hidden in the folds of her cloak and crept closer to the bed. She would have her answers tonight—one way or another.

She stepped up on to the platform of the bed

and reached out for his hand. Time seemed to slow down, taking on a hazy quality.

Suddenly, everything sped up horribly. The hand that had seemed so still, so restful, shot out and grabbed her wrist hard. Pain shot up her arm like a fire-tipped arrow and she cried out in shock.

He dragged her down on to the bed and his free hand clamped over her mouth, stifling her screams. She stared up at him, wide-eyed, suddenly sure that this was the end.

She couldn't see his face. The glow of the candle was behind him, casting a halo over the tumble of his sleep-rumpled dark hair, the gleam of the bare skin of his chest. His fingers tightened on her wrist until she went numb and let go of the dagger.

'Who are you?' he growled. 'Who sent you?'

Isabella shook her head. She could say nothing with his hand over her mouth. The movement dislodged the hood of her cloak and it fell away from her face.

Shock wiped away the fury on his face. 'Isabella?' he said roughly. His hand dropped from her mouth. 'What are you doing here? I thought perhaps it could be—but I would not have thought you so foolish.'

'I saw you!' she cried, all her anger and confusion tumbled together inside of her. 'In the cathedral. Matteo...'

Suddenly, the full horror of what had happened that day, and of what she had just done, crashed over her. A sob escaped her lips and she turned her head to the side so she couldn't see him. So he couldn't see her shameful tears.

'Isabella...' he said, his voice confused. 'You saw what happened?'

All she could do was nod.

'It was not what you thought,' he said. 'I swear that to you.'

'What else could it be? I saw you stab him. Were you somehow in league with the Pazzi?'

'Never. I only confronted Strozzi about—about something that happened a very long time ago. I tried to get answers. What happened was not planned.'

320   *Betrayed by His Kiss*

Not planned? Did that make the violence better or worse? In his surprise, his hold on her had loosened. She struck out at him with her fists on his bare shoulders, his chest, all the emotions of so many long days and longer nights flooding out of her. Once he had made her hope, made her want him, and now that made her hate him.

'I hate you!' she cried out. 'You were not what I thought. You were not—'

'Isabella!' He grabbed her hands and held them to the bed. 'Isabella, stop now and listen to me.'

But she was beyond listening. Beyond rational feelings. Too much had happened. 'You bastard! You...'

He bent his head and stopped her furious words with his mouth hard over hers. His tongue slid deep into her mouth and his hands were hard on her body as he dragged her closer to him.

Shocked, Isabella struggled against him, anger and desire battling inside of her. But his kiss was too overwhelming, too perfect, and she found herself holding on to him just as hard. Opening her mouth to him, tasting him deeply. The anger and the need flooded over them both, drowning them.

She slid her hands down his bare back, scratching his warm skin with her nails. He felt so hard, so strong, under her touch. He groaned and his kiss turned rough, nothing held back now. He forced her head back as his tongue plunged deeper, sliding over hers. She met him with equal fire, her arms wrapped around him, her nails digging into his back. She wanted the pleasure and the hurt all at once.

He tumbled her down onto the bed, among the rumpled blankets, and her skirts fell back from her legs. His mouth slid from her lips to her throat, her shoulder, the tip of his tongue tasting her skin. She shivered at the sensations every touch sent soaring through her.

'My god of the Underworld,' she whispered. 'If you stay here with me, you may never see sunlight again,' he moaned against her shoulder.

Somehow, she knew the darkness suited her now. Everything in the world had changed and she didn't know it any more. She didn't know herself. Her hand slid down his back, over his lean hip. He was naked under the bedclothes and she revelled in the feel of his bare skin. Her fingers skipped over his manhood. She had seen them before, on statues and in paintings, but it was wondrous to touch one. So hot and hard, like satin over burning steel.

He went perfectly still above her, his breath harsh in his throat. 'Do you like this?' she whispered.

'Too much,' he said hoarsely.

Isabella laughed, a glorious new feeling of power taking hold of her. She grew bolder, sliding her touch down his length, feeling him grow even harder under her hand.

But he pushed her away. She had no time to think, to wonder what might happen next. He pulled her gown away from her shoulders, leaving her body bare to him as the muslin fell from her back, her legs.

'You smell like roses,' he said.

She shivered as he bent over her again, touching his lips to her shoulder, the soft curve of her breast. His hands tumbled the pins from her hair, letting the heavy black mass fall free over his pillows. He stared at it as if entranced as he spread it over the pale linens.

Isabella could only watch him, unable to breathe or think. She could only feel. He was so very beautiful there above her. How could he ever be capable of evil? Nothing *felt* evil now. It was all too right. Too glorious.

His kiss traced over her bare body, light, teasing caresses, touching here and there, never lingering, until she moaned for more. Then he did something terribly shocking. He knelt between her legs and softly kissed the bare skin just at the top of her thigh.

'Orlando…' she gasped.

'Shhh,' he whispered against her. 'Just let me.'

He traced the seam of her womanhood with

the tip of his tongue before he plunged deep inside and tasted her very essence.

Isabella cried out at the pleasure. She had never imagined there could be anything like that in the world! When she came there that night, she didn't know what would happen, what she would do. She only knew she had to find answers. Now it seemed she had it—and it was nothing like she could have ever imagined.

Suddenly, she was not afraid any longer.

The pleasure threatened to overwhelm her. She caught his soft hair between her fingers and drew him up again so she could look into his eyes. She could read nothing there but a passion, a need, that answered her own.

He braced himself over her, his arms stiff at either side of her, and she could tell he held himself carefully so he wouldn't crush her with his strength. But she wanted him closer, so close she could lose herself in him and not have to face the real world again.

She wrapped her legs around his lean hips and tugged him closer to her, until their bodies were fitted together, softness to strength. His skin was so warm, damp and satin-smooth over his hard muscles. She traced a caress over his taut back, his bare backside, revelling in the way he felt. The strength of him. Godlike in truth, capable of such destruction and such pleasure all at once.

'Orlando,' she whispered, just to hear his name. She pressed her lips to his shoulder and tasted the salt of his sweat. How she craved the heat of him, to warm her after she had been cold for so long.

'Isabella,' he said roughly. He buried his face in the curve of her neck and she could feel his harsh breath against her. 'I know I should not do this. That I have wronged you too much. But I cannot hold back any longer…'

'I know.' She drew in a shuddering breath, and the scent of him was all around her, intoxicating. That dark essence of him she had craved ever since she first saw him.

He kissed her neck, his mouth open and hot, sliding over her shoulder again as if he wanted to taste her just as she did him. His mouth opened over the curve of her breast. 'I have never known anyone like you,' he said.

'Nor I you. Our sins must be meant for each other, then,' Isabella whispered, hardly knowing what she was saying. She could think no more.

He pushed aside the loose fall of her hair to kiss her ear. She felt the rush of his breath, the gentle bite of his teeth on her soft earlobe, and it made her shiver. She arched up into him, her hips brushing the hardness of his erection. The proof of his desire for her.

His kiss pressed to that sensitive spot just below her ear, making her gasp. 'Do you like that?' he said against her.

'I feel as if I'm falling,' she said truthfully. Falling down and down, into a place she didn't recognize at all.

'I will catch you. Just let yourself fall, *bella*.'

So she did. She dared to leap out into the unknown into the sparkling mist. She traced her hand down his naked chest, his back, feeling every inch of his skin. He shuddered when she touched his manhood again. It hardened even more and she closed her fingers around him.

He shuddered and pushed her hand away. Before she could protest, he touched *her*, his thumb tracing the wet core of her, making her cry out. She spread her legs wider, letting him feel all of her desire.

This had to be, she knew that. Fate had been leading them here ever since they met, whatever came afterwards. Orlando seemed to feel that, too.

He gently parted her folds with his fingertips as he knelt between her legs. His hips gave a twist and she felt a sudden stretch and burn as he slowly entered her. She gasped at the unfamiliar friction, that new sensation of fullness at their joining.

'I am sorry,' he whispered. He went very still, his arms rigid as he held himself balanced above her. His back tightened as if he would pull back from her.

'No!' she cried. 'Don't leave.' Her legs closed

hard around him, holding him with her so she could feel more and more. Feel them fully together at last.

The ache was fading as her body grew accustomed to his, leaving only that delicious fullness and a faint, faraway glimmer of something she could not quite grasp. Something wondrous, that she sensed she could only have with him.

He drew back one slow, tantalizing inch at a time, almost sliding out of her before he flexed his hips and plunged deep again.

'Oh,' she gasped as he did this again and again, moving faster and faster. That tiny seed of pleasure inside her grew, flowering and expanding until her whole body seemed to come to fiery life, ignited by the feel of his body in hers, joined to her in every way. She instinctively learned his rhythm, moving with him, the two of them perfectly together.

The whole planet seemed narrowed to only his body in hers. Behind her tightly closed eyes, she saw sparks of gold and silver, shimmering, and a humming began in her ears, like the music from the dance. She just wanted more and more, wanted this to go on for ever.

Then all her thoughts and feelings, everything she was, flew apart in an explosion of fiery stars. She felt like she was soaring into the sky, her old self burning up until she could emerge anew.

Above her, Orlando shouted out her name as his back arched. He pulled out of her and she felt the damp warmth of his seed against her hip. He collapsed beside her on to the bed, their arms and legs entangled.

Isabella slowly sank back down to earth, those stars still scattering around her. She had never felt so light, so tired, so very confused. She did not know what would happen tomorrow, or even in the next moment, but being with Orlando had been inevitable.

Beside her, she heard the ragged rhythm of his breath, the heave of his chest as his own release slowed. She opened her eyes and rolled carefully on to her side to study him in the flickering candlelight. His eyes were half-closed and he did not smile. This was not a moment for smiling, though. It seemed to be a moment when everything changed.

'Do you still want to kill me, Isabella?' he asked hoarsely.

Shocked by his words, she shook her head. 'I do not know,' she answered truthfully. 'I do not know what I want now, what I should do. Once I thought I knew what was right. But now…'

'What is right is always complicated,' he said.

And so it was. Everything that had happened in Florence had turned all she thought she knew upside down and now she was sure she lived in a different world. An Underworld, where he was the lord.

But her body felt sure that what had just happened was *right*. She softly kissed the corner of his mouth. 'I cannot kill you tonight. I must return to my room.'

'Not yet, surely. It is still deepest night and there is much I have to tell you,' Orlando answered.

Isabella propped herself up on her elbow to

study his beautiful, starkly elegant face. How she wished she could read him, as she could other people. But he hid from her artist's eye all too well. 'I think there must be.'

He pushed himself up off the bed and walked naked to a table by the window, laid out with a platter of fruit and ewers of wine, silver goblets. She studied the powerful line of his back, his long legs, and she longed for her sketchbook. Maybe in art she could capture him, but she feared even then he would be far from her. Unreadable.

He came back to the bed, two goblets in his hand, and he handed one to her. She sipped at the wine, which was soft on her raw throat, and tried not to look at him. Looking at him was much too overwhelming. What had just happened between them still seemed too raw, too unreal.

'You will know the truth soon enough, Isabella, I promise you,' he said.

Isabella tried to nod, but suddenly her head felt too heavy to hold up. The room grew blurry and the goblet fell from her suddenly numb fingers. Orlando caught it and she felt his arms come around her to ease her back to the bed.

'I am sorry,' he said.

Then she realized what had happened. That he was truly a villain after all and she had been the greatest of fools. She tried to cry out, but the room faded to deepest black.

Chapter Eighteen

Isabella groaned as bright light sparkled just beyond her closed eyes, forcing her up out of the peaceful darkness of sleep. Her whole body felt so heavy and she wanted to sink back down into dreams again. Into memories of kisses…

She tried to roll over, to burrow down into the warm blankets, but a hand on her shoulder wouldn't let her.

'Isabella,' someone called and it sounded as if the voice came from a very long way away. She moaned and shook them away, but they just called out to her again. 'Isabella!'

She pried open her eyes and stared up at a low, whitewashed ceiling, criss-crossed with dark beams. An unfamiliar ceiling, not her small bedroom at home, or the embroidered hangings of Caterina's house. Where *was* she?

Then it all came flooding back, memories tumbling through her mind. Orlando's chamber, his hand hard over her mouth, the anger and grief and raw need. His body sliding over hers. And the wine that had made her so very dizzy...

The wine! That deep-dyed villain. He had put something into her wine and she had been the veriest fool to drink it.

Isabella sat up with a gasp. The blanket wrapped around her tumbled down and she saw she wore her rumpled masquerade costume. Its diaphanous cream-and-apricot folds looked absurd in the daylight. She jerked the blanket up over her shoulders and spun around to face the voice that called her name.

Orlando stood there beside the narrow bed she lay on. He wore his usual black garments, his hair brushed back from his brow. His jaw was darkened with morning whiskers, but otherwise he looked as austere and elegant as always—damn him. He watched her warily, a small frown on his lips.

Isabella quickly glanced around the room and found it was small and stark, with only one arched window, and a stool and washstand besides the bed. A flaking fresco of a Madonna with a bowed head, muffled in a pale blue robe, stared down at her from above the window.

Was this a prison of some sort? Had he locked her in here as punishment for what she had done? How dare he do such a thing, when he had driven her to such evil thoughts in the first place!

'You drugged me,' she cried. She pushed herself off the bed, too quickly, and a cold wave of dizziness broke over her.

Orlando reached out for her arm, his hand warm on her bare skin. She shook him away, but he wouldn't leave. He gently made her sit back down on the bed, standing over her until she was even dizzier with the clean, citrus scent of him.

'I am sorry, Isabella,' he said, too quietly, too

gently. ''Twas only an herb to help you sleep, nothing harmful. I could think of no other way to persuade you to come here with me and time is short.'

'And where is here?' Isabella said, her mind whirling with memories of all that had happened last night. Confusion over what was happening now. 'What is happening?'

'This is the convent of St Clare. I promise you, no harm will come to you here.'

'Why should I believe you?' She stared up into his eyes, trying to read the truth there. All she could see was how dark a green they were now, how solemn, and somehow that frightened her. 'Why did you bring me here? To make me do penance for trying to kill you?'

Orlando gave a harsh laugh. 'If anyone should do penance, it is surely me. I kept the truth from you too long, Isabella, and for selfish reasons.'

'What is the truth?' She felt she had lost it so long ago, the truth, and she did not know where to seek it now.

He held out his hand and gave a wry smile

when she looked at it suspiciously. 'Come, let me show you something.'

She stood up carefully. She ignored his hand and held the blanket close around her. She surely had no choice but to listen to him now. Things were never as they seemed in the up-side-down world she had inhabited since she left her father's house. Perhaps, just perhaps, his words could turn them right-side-up again.

If she dared to believe him, to even listen to him. Everyone had hidden things from her for too long. Why should now, here, be any different?

Yet she remembered last night, all too well. The feeling of such lightness, such strange safety when he held her in his arms. The truth she tasted in his kiss. The way nothing else seemed to matter for only that one hour. Surely that could not all be a lie?

And surely he would not lie now, in a sacred place like this, and endanger his soul further. Even villains could not do that.

He led her to the small window and she went

Betrayed by His Kiss

up on tiptoe to peer outside. She found herself looking down on a garden, a small, pretty, pale green space of neat pathways and stone statues of placid saints. Just beyond were the arches and covered corridors of a cloister walk, sunlight shimmering on the creamy-yellow bricks.

A group of nuns in their dark habits walked there, hands folded before them and their heads bent together as they whispered. Ahead of them skipped a little girl in a white dress. Her red-gold hair sparkled as she danced and spun. She seemed like a spirit of the light and air, landed in the dark, calm quiet of the cloister.

'That's the child I saw with you before,' Isabella blurted.

She felt Orlando watching her. 'You saw her with me before?'

'At the *palazzo*.' She remembered the way Orlando and the child smiled at each other. 'Is she your daughter? Is that what you are telling me?'

'My daughter? Nay. That is—Maria *is* my child now, I take care of her the best I can, for she has no one else. She is my niece. But I fear I must tell you her natural father was your cousin, Matteo Strozzi.'

Matteo? Shocked, Isabella's gaze flew up to Orlando's face. She read there only solemn stillness, only the truth. How was it Orlando took Matteo's child into his care, treating her so tenderly, and yet he could kill her father? Why then...?

Why had Matteo never spoken of the child? She looked back to the little girl, who was picking a bouquet of flowers. Isabella suddenly realized the child's hair was the same beautiful colour as that of Caterina and Matteo. She was so lovely, surely a prize any father could claim. Even bastard children could make alliances. Could be loved.

'Tell me all,' she whispered.

''Tis not a pretty tale,' he said, his voice sad, wary.

'Neither is anything that has happened of late,' she said.

He gave a grim nod. 'Very true. Maria's mother was my younger sister. Our father betrothed her to a neighbour before he died, but she did not like her fiancé. She had—romantic dreams. And a trip to Florence before her wedding proved to be a terrible mistake.'

'So she fell in love with Matteo?' Isabella demanded, remembering the romantic poems Caterina read. How their tragic tales unfolded. 'And you had to revenge yourself on him for stealing her from her hated fiancé?'

'You have been reading much, I see,' Orlando said. 'And you are partially correct, but I fear the story is not so romantic. Maria Lorenza fell in love with Matteo. She had never been away from the countryside and she was dazzled by Florence, as so many are. Strozzi seduced her, and when she found herself with child he abandoned her. Laughed at her, she claimed. At the time he was betrothed to a lady of the Riario family, with connections to the pope. He would not ruin that for a country maiden. And my father denounced her as well, before he died.'

Isabella stared down at the beautiful, laughing child and tried to imagine the girl's mother.

Beautiful, young, despairing. Her life in ruins because she had trusted, loved, in the wrong place. Alone and frightened. It was too easy to picture. Could it be true?

'What happened to her?' she asked quietly.

'She came to me for help.'

Isabella looked up at him in surprise. 'She came to you? Her brother, who would surely want to avenge family honour?'

Orlando's face was stark, unreadable, as he also watched the child. 'We were friends as well as siblings. Maria Lorenza was a sweet spirit who never deserved to be dealt with in such a foul way. Someone had to take care of her and her innocent child.'

'And you did that,' Isabella said doubtfully. How many men, so careful of their honour, would do such a thing? And yet…yet Orlando was not as most men were. She had seen ample proof of that.

'Our long-dead mother's aunt was abbess here then and I asked her to take in Maria Lorenza and help her bring the baby into the world.'

'Is she here now? Maria Lorenza?' Isabella asked, half-afraid she would be.

He frowned and, before he turned away, Isabella thought she glimpsed a flash of some deep, barely restrained emotion in his eyes. Anger? Sorrow? She, who was so used to reading emotions and putting them into paint, could not be sure with him.

'She died soon after Maria was born,' he said brusquely. 'Even her baby could not tie her to life after what Matteo Strozzi did to her. Her heart was shattered. She took poison.'

'Poison!' Isabella gasped in shock. 'She did away with herself? Here, in this sacred place?'

Orlando's mouth hardened. 'My aunt managed to conceal it so Maria Lorenza could be buried in the sisters' churchyard, but it surely was no accident.'

'And you have taken care of the little girl ever since?'

'Someone had to. She is innocent of her parents' sins.'

Isabella looked back to the child and remembered how Orlando had held her tiny hand. How they smiled together. He was so tender with her, so gentle, and yet he had killed Matteo in the frenzy of the bloodlust that had erupted in the cathedral. She had come here to revenge that act. How could the two be reconciled?

She remembered her father's books, his mutterings of honour and honesty, the teachings of the ancient philosophers that were meant to guide men's path. How had Orlando come to be on this very path now, where he could find her? What was she meant to see? To know?

Her life had never prepared her for such a thing and she feared now to take a wrong step once again.

'So you planned your revenge towards Matteo for so long?' she said.

'I did hate him, verily,' Orlando admitted. 'How could I not? But I wanted him to confess to what he had done, repent for it. He merely laughed, just as Maria Lorenza said he once did with her. She was as nothing to him, even in memory. He wanted to fight in the cathedral, as so many others did. So we fought.'

'I saw you kill him,' Isabella whispered. Every time she closed her eyes, she saw again that dagger.

Matteo had been her cousin, aye. Yet how much did she know of him? She pressed her hand to her lips as she tried to think, to remember. His careless laughter with his friends, Caterina's worried eyes as she watched him.

Could he have done this terrible thing? Surely he could; men were capable of so much evil, as she had seen too well in Florence. But had he?

'How can I know what is true?' she said. 'What is justice?'

Orlando removed a small parchment packet from within the folds of his cloak. Silently, he pressed it into her hands.

'These are letters Maria Lorenza sent me. I once thought I would never show them to anyone, that I would burn them, but you deserve to know all of her tale,' he said solemnly. He stepped back and gave her a sad smile. 'One of the sisters will bring you fresh clothes and some food. I will leave you now. I have taken too much from you, I fear, and I beg you to forgive me.'

Isabella watched, stunned, as he turned and went to the door. As he reached for the latch, she cried out, 'You are leaving?' It hardly seemed true that he could be gone so quickly.

He didn't turn around. 'I must. You need to think about all of this for yourself, my sweet Isabella. I am sorry I had to bring you here like this, tell you of these tawdry things. If I could, I would have kept you always as we were for those moments in Florence—so sure of the beauty of the world.'

He glanced back at her then, with that sad, heartbreaking smile on his beautiful face. 'You gave me the greatest gift, Isabella. You gave me a peace I had never known. I only wish I could have given you that in return. Know I am here for you if ever you need me. If ever you can forgive me.'

He left, shutting the door softly behind him.

Isabella instinctively started to run after him, to demand he tell her more, but something in his very sadness held her back. She had never felt so lonely as she did in that moment.

She looked out the window again and saw the little girl sitting on a stone bench with one of the sisters, her head bent over an open book. Her fair hair glowed and she did look so much like Matteo in that instant.

Isabella turned away and opened the first letter in her hand. It was a short note, the ink blotted as if the writer had cried over it as she laboured to make the words. The letters were carefully formed, as if Maria had not been much educated. But her emotions were stark on the page as she poured out her heartbreak and fear to her only friend. To Orlando.

The tale was as Orlando had said, only sadder. More despairing. Isabella could feel the girl's heartbreak. The letters looked real, felt real in every way. Surely they could not be forged, part of some elaborate plan.

Stunned by the sadness of it all, Isabella almost dropped the letters to the stone floor as remorse overcame her.

She ran to the door. She didn't know where she was going, what she would do, she only knew she had to find Orlando. Throw her arms around him, tell him she would not doubt her own feelings again. That she would never let him go.

But as she swung open the door, she found a startled nun standing there with a plain blue-wool gown over her arm. Isabella realized she could not go dashing around a convent dressed as she was, so she submitted to a quick *toilette* from the smiling sister. Yet she fidgeted, filled with so very many questions, so many doubts and emotions she could not make sense of it all.

When she was finally respectably dressed, she dashed down to the garden, only to find the little girl gone. Orlando was nowhere to be seen. Only the letters she clutched in her hand proved he had been there at all.

She ran to the edge of the garden and peered down the pathways. He wasn't there.

'Are you Signorina Isabella?' someone asked softly.

Isabella whirled around to find a shyly smiling young nun. 'I am.'

She held out a folded letter. 'Signor Landucci left this for you. I was meant to wait to give it to you, but you look as if you need it now, I fear.'

Isabella took the note and the nun melted away as suddenly as she had appeared. Isabella broke the wax that sealed the note and read it quickly. Surely he had written it before he even brought her there, for the wax had hardened, the ink dried.

My beautiful Isabella,

My secret is in your hands now, to do with as you must. You have truly given me a great gift in a life I fear has been misspent. You gave me peace and beauty, the vision of a true life. Now I give it back to you and beg you to take it. The sisters will see that you are taken safely back to your father's house, as I am taking Maria to safety now.

*If you still wish to take your revenge, then
I will return for your answer soon.*
  My life is yours.
  Orlando

Isabella crumpled the note, choking on a cry that would not escape. He was gone now. He had given her his secret, his very life, and that of his child. He trusted her. But how could she now trust herself?

'Where are we going, Uncle Orlando?' Maria asked brightly as he lifted her into the boat that would carry them away from Fiencosole.

Home, he almost answered. Yet where was home for them? He could not go back to Florence, to the empty life he had led there. His revenge on Matteo Strozzi was complete, yet it was naught but a hollow shell. Isabella had changed everything, had changed the whole world. And now he had to try to find a way to remake it all over again, without her.

'We are going on an adventure, my little one,'

he said, making himself laugh so she wouldn't realize anything was amiss. He had to take care of Maria now and she looked at him with far too much worry in her eyes for such a little girl. 'Won't that be grand?'

Maria clapped her hands and giggled. 'Like in the stories Sister Benedicta reads to me? About the knight who seeks his princess, his one true jewel, even through enchanted forests and stormy seas?'

'That does not sound like something a nun like Sister Benedicta should be reading,' Orlando said as he loaded Maria's cases after her. Indeed, it sounded as if the good sister shared a love of romantic poetry with Lucretia. The prince's one rare jewel, which he sought after in vain all his misspent life.

Orlando looked back to the white towers of Fiencosole, rising over the thick walls that lined the river. He did leave a jewel there, the one thing that might have truly redeemed him.

He had left his life, and Maria's, too, in Isabella's paint-stained hands. Now his quest had to begin again. Once he saw Maria safe, perhaps he could go questing again, and his jewel would hold out her hand to him in forgiveness.

If that hand did not hold a dagger instead. Orlando smiled wryly to remember how fierce his gentle, artistic Isabella could truly be. How fiery in her passion.

Aye—his quest was not yet ended.

'Come, Maria,' he said, swinging himself into the boat. 'Adventure awaits!'

Chapter Nineteen

'In a short time passes every great rain; and the warmth makes disappear the snows and ice that make the rivers look so proud...'

'You have much improved, Veronica,' Isabella said as she bent her head over her sketchbook, trying to capture and hold the last light of the day.

She glanced up and saw her father's villa in the peachy sunset of a late summer's day. The green shutters were thrown open and maidservants leaned out of the windows, laughing together in the calm moment before they had to finish making supper. Everything looked lovely, pastoral—familiar.

Her father sat at his table beneath the shade

of the trees, his books piled around him, his white hair too long and flying around his head in the breeze. He had forgotten his hat again. Mena called to him from the doorway, but he didn't look up. He was lost in his own world.

It was as if nothing at all had changed while she was gone. Yet nothing was the same.

She looked back down at her sketchbook. Hades sat on his throne, surrounded by his dark courtiers at a banquet in the Underworld. He watched their revels with a solemn, unreadable expression on his austerely elegant features. He was part of that world of shadows, yet he was completely alone.

The grey-and-black lines of the drawing seemed to come alive in her mind, a swirl of colours, sudden bolts of light amid the shadows. She had learned much from her too-brief hours in Signor Botticelli's studio. A scene like this could not be one of realism, but of sensuality, emotion, ethereal fancy. It was all about Hades and his deep, profound loneliness. His beauty.

Hades. Isabella felt the chilly touch of sad-

ness that came to her so often now. It had been
weeks since she and Orlando parted in Fiencosole, yet still she saw his face so clearly in her
mind, the deep sadness in his eyes. At night
she lay awake in the moonlight and remembered how it felt when he touched her. How for
those moments when they were together everything seemed so perfect.

And how horribly it had all been shattered.

'Signorina Isabella!' Veronica called. 'Mena
says you must come to supper now.'

'I will be there anon,' Isabella answered. Life
there at her father's house did seem to go on
as usual, with the farm and the meals and the
washing, the books and the letters. She tried to
go on, too, tried to pretend she was the same
Isabella who had once left for Florence. But
sometimes she thought she would crack with
the effort, like one of the ancient statues in the
garden.

Would she ever see Orlando again? Or were
they fated to only have those few moments in
Florence? That one night? A glimpse of love

and beauty that could not be, because the world around them was so very ugly.

At least she had her art. She could see Orlando again there and he would never change. He was there, in his eternal Underworld, and in her dreams at night.

She carefully closed her sketchbook and followed Veronica back to the house. The maids had left off their gossiping at the windows and were laying out the plates for supper on a table beneath the trees. Her father was still bent over his books and he would be until Mena forced him to eat.

But he looked up as Isabella kissed his cheek and he frowned. 'You look tired, my dearest,' he said. 'I fear your time in Florence has not done you any good at all.'

Isabella smiled at him and carefully smoothed his hair. She couldn't tell her father that her sleepless nights were because she could not stop thinking of Orlando. No one here knew of him and she had no words to describe him anyway.

Mena bustled out of the house, a tureen of

steaming soup in her hands. She had asked nothing since Isabella sent her home from Florence so suddenly, but she always watched her carefully. Always brought her cups of spiced wine at night.

'She is home now, *signor*, where she can rest, and that is all that matters. We will soon fatten her up, too,' Mena said.

Isabella laughed and turned to help her father put away his books. Suddenly, far down the overgrown path at the garden gate, she glimpsed a tall, dark-clad figure.

She froze, sure she was dreaming yet again. She blinked hard and saw he was still there.

'Isabella!' she heard her father call, but she could hardly hear him. She walked slowly down the path, afraid if she moved too fast he would vanish. But soon she found herself running, faster and faster.

She'd thought she would never see him again and yet there he was. Orlando. Like a dream dropped suddenly into her real life.

'Isabella,' he said as she stumbled to a halt.

His voice sounded strange, hoarse and cracked. He held out his hand to her and it trembled.

'Orlando, how did you find me?' she cried. 'What are you doing here…?' Then she really looked at him and her throat went dry.

His doublet was unlaced, his white linen shirt damp with the sweat that cast a faint gleam over his skin. Under the sun-bronze, he was alarmingly pale. His hair was brushed back from his brow in tangled waves. His eyes glittered.

'You shouldn't come closer,' he said. ''Tis a fever.'

'Nay!' Isabella whispered, all her joy at seeing him again vanishing into a cold fear. How could she lose him now?

He swayed and she ran forward to take him in her arms as he fell. She gently cradled his head in her lap, aghast as she studied his beautiful face. He was so very warm against her.

'What happened?' she said. She gently smoothed his hair back.

'I left Maria at an abbey nearby. We were to leave for Venice—but I had to see you again,' he gasped. 'To explain—why I left you. I never meant…'

'Shh, be quiet now,' Isabella urged him. Her throat was tight with fear. 'I know why we had to part, too. I was so wrong. I…'

His shaking hand reached up and gently touched her cheek. 'Isabella. I should have told you the moment we met. But I wanted to hold on to you just a little longer. I was selfish.'

His hand fell away and his eyes closed.

'Orlando,' she called. But he didn't say anything else.

'Isabella, what is this?' she heard Mena say. Isabella looked up at her, confused and very, very frightened.

''Tis Orlando,' she said, numb. 'He's come back to me. He's ill.'

'Well, we cannot leave him here, can we, lamb? You carry his shoulders and I will get his feet. Veronica can run into the village for the physician.'

Something in Mena's crisp, matter-of-fact

tone shook Isabella out of her cold fear. She nodded and hefted Orlando up in her arms.

Even though he was tall, with such lean, hard muscles, they managed to lift him up between them and carried him down the path towards the house.

'What is happening?' Isabella's father said, obviously bewildered, but they went past him and into the cool, dim quiet of the house. They laid him on a bench near the stairs and Mena hurried off, muttering about fetching water and blankets.

Isabella leaned over Orlando, examining his ashen face, his pale lips. He was so quiet now, but his brow was creased, his jaw clenched as if he fought fierce battles in his fever dreams.

Her beloved. Isabella couldn't stop staring at him, willing him to live. If she had not been so foolish, so naive in the ways of the world…

But she could not regret the past now. She could only keep him with her now.

She took his hand tightly in hers, raising his cold fingers to her lips. He tasted of the faint salt of sweat, but underneath there was still that dark, familiar sweetness of her Orlando, the essence she remembered so well from their precious night together. The passionate, vivid, burningly alive man who had been in her bed. That had caressed her, brought her such delight. She couldn't lose him now.

'Don't leave me again, Orlando,' she whispered. 'Please, please, stay with me. Let us find our way back to each other.'

His eyes fluttered open. For an instant, they were clouded, their sea-green colour darkened. But then they focused on her and they sharpened. His hand tightened on hers.

'Isabella?' he said hoarsely.

'Yes, it's me,' she answered, trying to smile. 'You are in my home now. You will be well soon.'

He shook his head. 'You're not a dream.'

'Nay, I am not a dream. I'm real. This is real.'

'No, you hate me now.' Suddenly his eyes closed again and his back arched, as if in a spasm of pain.

'Here,' Mena said, kneeling beside Isabella. A maidservant hovered behind her with a basin of steaming water, and Mena held a small bottle of a dark elixir. She unstoppered it. 'Hold his head.'

As Isabella cradled him against her, Mena carefully counted drops into his mouth. He grew quiet again and Mena gently bathed his face with the warm water. 'We will soon have him well, my lamb. You will see.'

Something in Mena's quiet voice steadied Isabella, but still she was afraid. Was it all much too late?

'Orlando! Orlando, wake up now, please.'

Orlando pried open his gritty eyes, his hand instinctively reaching for his dagger. The last thing he remembered was leaving Maria at the abbey outside Isabella's village while he went to find Isabella's house, to beg her forgiveness. The realization that he could not be without her, even as he knew he was not good for her. He had come near her house and then the damnable weakness, the heat, overcame him…

'Orlando, look at me!' a desperate voice cried and he felt a cool touch on his cheek.

Isabella's face swam into view above him, a hazy corona of light around her. Her eyes looked red-rimmed and exhausted, his black hair loose. But her smile was beautiful as she caressed his face.

Was she part of his fever dream, or had he truly found her? He dared not hope.

'Am I dead?' he said, his throat dry and aching.

Her reluctant smile widened. 'You cannot be, for I am no angel. You are in my father's house. Do you remember coming here?'

He nodded. He did remember the surge of hope in knowing she was near again. And here she was. He could feel her hand on his skin, smell her perfume. Her eyes held no hatred now as they looked down at him.

Slowly, he became aware of other things. He lay on a comfortable bed, with clean sheets and feather pillows. Above him was a green-velvet canopy and candlelight cast strange shadows on the embroidered patterns. A window was open, letting in a warm summer breeze that smelled of sweet flowers. There was a feeling of profound safety, or peace, there, one he hadn't known in a very long time.

And it was all because of the woman who held his hand now. His rare jewel.

He clutched at her hand, feeling her fingers curl around his. He never wanted to lose that again, if he could only persuade her to stay with him.

'Is anyone else ill here?' he managed to ask.

She shook her head. 'Only you. Mena and I have been looking after you and now thankfully your fever has quite broken.'

She eased her hand from his and reached for a basin of water on the table beside the bed. She soaked a cloth in it and gently bathed his face in its lavender-scented coolness.

'Have you forgiven my sins?' he murmured. 'That was why I sought out this place, to beg you to forgive me. I found I could not leave until I did.'

Her hand grew slower and a frown flickered over her face. 'You did what you had to for that poor child and for her mother. My cousin did a cruel thing and now he has paid for it. But so has his sister, who was as innocent as your Maria Lorenza. I cannot live my life in that way any longer. My taste of it in Florence has sickened me.'

'Isabella...' Orlando began, but the deep sadness of her face stopped his words. He hardly knew what he could say to make things better anyway.

'You should rest,' she said, her voice soft and so, so sad. He would do anything at all to take that sadness away from her, for ever.

But then she smiled and he glimpsed the wide-eyed innocence that had so drawn him to her when he first glimpsed her in Florence.

'I don't want to rest,' he said. 'I feared we would never be together again. I just want to look at you.'

Her smile widened. 'And I want you to be well again. We have so much to do…'

'Such as this?' He could no longer resist. He reached up and threaded his fingers in her black, silken hair to tug her down closer to him. He claimed her lips in a hard, frantic kiss, a kiss he poured all his dreams into. She tasted cool and sweet. She tasted of Isabella. Of *life* and light.

For an instant, she stiffened as if she would draw away, but then she melted into him. She moaned softly, and kissed him back, just as he had dreamed she would.

It was like coming home at last.

'Lie down here beside me.'

Isabella smiled at Orlando's words and gently stretched out beside him in the blankets. His arms came around her, and for the first time in so many weeks she felt safe. Things felt right at long last.

She knew the world was still out there. The ugliness she had glimpsed in Florence. But now all that seemed so far away. Orlando was here with her, healthy and whole, and they could refashion the future together. It was hazy and mysterious, yet somehow, in the midst of it all, they had found each other. For that one perfect moment, it was all that mattered.

She studied his face, every inch of it, greedily. She had thought of him every day since she returned home, gone over every word they once shared, every touch and kiss. Now he was really here, with her again.

His own stare roved hungrily over her face, as if he had missed her too. What had happened when they were apart? Had he really missed her, thought of her?

The thought made something crack inside of her heart and all the longing, all the fear, all the love, flew free. She pressed one swift, soft kiss to his lips, then another and another, teasing him until he half laughed, half groaned and pulled her even closer against him. So close nothing could come between them at all.

'Orlando,' she whispered. 'Are you well enough? Should we…?'

In answer, he moaned against her lips and deepened the kiss, his tongue lightly seeking hers, and Isabella was lost in him all over again. The way it was in Florence, the hot need that always rose in her when he touched her, surrounded them all over again like a wall of flame that shut out the rest of the world. She wanted only to be this close to him again, always. To be part of him and make him part of her.

She had questioned, worried, wondered for so long. Now she wanted only to be with Orlando again, to feel as only he could make her feel. To know there was hope in the future when they were together, that it was not a dream.

Orlando's lips slid away from hers and he pressed tiny, fleeting kisses to her cheek, the line of her jaw, that oh-so-sensitive spot just below her ear. The spot that had always made her feel so wild when he kissed it. She shivered at the warm rush of his breath over her skin.

She laughed breathlessly and wrapped her arms around his shoulders to try and hold herself straight. She feared she would fall down and down into love with him again, and be lost for good this time.

'Isabella,' he whispered hoarsely, pressing his lips to her hair, 'I need you so much. When I thought I had lost you, I went mad.'

She rested her cheek on the curve of his neck and inhaled deeply of the wonderful, familiar scent of his skin. This had always been the one true thing between them, the way their bodies knew one another, craved one another. Said things they never could in words.

And she knew in that moment she had to let go of her fears. Silently, she took his hand in hers again and pressed a soft kiss to his callused palm. She only wanted to feel the way Orlando could make her feel. She wanted to feel close to him again.

She lay back on the cushions and looked at him in the shadows. His eyes glowed and his face looked taut and intent with the desire she could tell he tried to hold back. She raised her arms up to him in a silent gesture of welcome.

'Isabella—are you sure?' he said roughly.

'Shh, Orlando,' she whispered. She wanted no words now. Words only shattered the spell she wanted to weave around them. To try to repair some of the damage they'd done in the name of revenge and false honour. Their love was the only honour.

She reached up and drew the pins from her hair, letting it coil around her shoulders. He'd always liked her hair, and she watched his eyes darken as he studied her every movement. Feeling bolder, she shook her hair down her back and slowly unlaced the neckline of her gown. The cool air brushed over her bared shoulders.

'Isabella!' he moaned, rubbing his hand over his eyes. 'What are you thinking now?'

'Please, Orlando,' she said. She swallowed her fear and smiled up at him. 'I want you. Don't you want me?'

'Of course I do. I've always wanted you more than anything in the world. But I—'

Whatever he wanted to say was lost when he caught her up in his arms and kissed her, passionately, deeply, nothing held back any longer.

Isabella felt as if her soul caught fire. She had to be closer, closer. Her touch, light, trembling, learned his body all over again. The smooth, damp heat of his skin, the light, coarse hair dusted over his chest, the tight muscles of his stomach, his lean hips.

The hard ridge of his erection, straining against the cloth of the sheet that lay over him. Oh, yes—she remembered *that* very well. As they kissed, falling down into the humid heat of need, she felt his hands sliding over her shoulders, releasing the fastenings of her gown and drawing it away.

She kicked the skirt down and laughed as they slid together, skin to skin, the silken length of her hair twirling around them to bind them together. He pressed his open, hot breath to her neck and all thought vanished into pure sensation.

Isabella closed her eyes and let herself just feel. Feel his hand on her hip, his mouth on the curve of her breast. She ran her hands over his strong shoulders, the arc of his back, and couldn't believe they were here, together like this again. Her legs parted as she felt the weight of his body lower against her.

He reached between them to touch her again and then at last he pressed against her, thrusting inside. It had been so long since they were together that at first it stung a bit, but that was nothing to the wonderful sensation of being joined with him again.

She arched up into him, wrapping her arms and legs around him to hold him with her.

'Isabella,' he groaned and slowly moved inside her again. Deeper, harder, until there was only pleasure. A wondrous delight that grew and grew like a sparkling cloud, spreading all through her.

She cried out, overcome by the wonder of it. How had she lived all those months without that, without him?

Above her, she felt Orlando's body go tense, his head arched back. 'Isabella!' he shouted out and his voice echoed inside of her, all around her.

And then she exploded, too, consumed by how he made her feel. She clung to him, feeling as if she tumbled down from the sky.

Long moments later, once she could breathe again, she slowly opened her eyes. For an instant, she was startled to find the familiar old room and not some new, enchanted glade. Orlando lay next to her, his arm tight around her waist. His eyes were closed, his body sprawled around hers in the way she remembered so well. Almost as if they had never been apart at all.

She closed her eyes again and fell back down into the sweet, drowning warmth of being near him all over again.

'Can you truly forgive me, Isabella, for all I have done?' he said quietly.

She pressed her face to his shoulder and breathed him in deeply. 'Do you—love me, Orlando?'

His breath caught and for a second she feared she had said too much. Shattered the delicacy of that precious moment. But then he spoke. 'I love you so much, Isabella. I have since I first saw you. I know I can never be free of it. I am yours, to do with as you will, for always.'

With those wondrous words, she let herself cry at last. They were joyful tears, as everything she had loved and feared came true at last. Orlando was here, alive. And he loved her.

She tilted back her head to smile up at him and he gently cupped her cheek in his hand.

'As I am yours. I love you, too,' she said 'I will forgive you everything, if you will promise never to leave me again.'

'Never,' he said firmly. 'You are bound to me for ever.'

For ever. Surely there were no sweeter words. He kissed her, his lips soft, sweet, hungry, and in that kiss she tasted all that love could truly mean. The pain of the past was gone and all they had was each other.

They belonged together. For ever.

Epilogue

Three months later

'Is Isabella going to paint a portrait of the *king*?'

Isabella laughed as she listened to little Maria whisper to Orlando. She sat perched on a coil of rope, her sketchbook balanced on her knees as the ship plunged through the waves. She was sketching her father as he argued with a group of sailors over his volume of Pliny, trying to explain his concept of natural history.

She could hardly believe all that had happened in the last weeks. She and Orlando had married and fetched Maria from her abbey sanctuary. Life at the villa was peaceful enough, an idyll of sunny days together, but the news from

Florence grew worse. Lorenzo de Medici had summoned his allies to help him hunt down all the Pazzi conspirators who had fled. There were executions every week and Pazzi houses were destroyed. It would not be safe to remain in Italy for a time.

So Orlando's kinsman at Fiencosole, along with Botticelli and Signor Salle, gained a commission for Isabella at the English court of King Edward. There she would paint his courtiers for a year and help the world see England as a truly powerful, peaceful place.

To her surprise, her father refused to be left behind. 'When would I have another chance to meet such strange people as the English?' he had insisted as he packed his books. 'I would love to learn the opinion of the philosophers there, if there are any...'

And of course Mena had to come to be nursemaid to Maria, who had become like a daughter to them all.

So Isabella was launched on another adventure, her whole family with her. As she lifted her face to the fresh, cool salt spray, she felt the excitement of a whole new beginning wash over her.

'Not the king himself, *bella*, but the people at his court,' Isabella said with a smile for Maria. 'Their beautiful clothes, their palaces...'

'Their jewels?' Maria cried. 'You must show their jewels.'

'Of course I must.' Isabella held out her arms, and Maria ran into them. She clambered up onto Isabella's lap, reaching for the sketchbook to study the charcoal images there.

'I like how you did Grandpapa's beard there,' Maria said with a thoughtful frown. 'But his hair is all wrong...'

'An artist already!' Orlando said. He kissed Isabella's cheek and his arms came around her and the child, holding them safe even on the wide sea. Even in the new world they faced together.

'She will be a brilliant artist,' Isabella said, leaning back into his strength and warmth of her husband. 'And she will love England, I am sure.'

'We shall all be together there. A new life for us.'

'So we shall.' *For ever.* That was what Isabella kept telling herself as she looked to the horizon. She had her husband, her family, her love, right now. And they were hers. For always.

* * * * *

Author Note

I was first inspired to write Isabella and Orlando's story when I had a yucky cold and spent the weekend lounging around on the couch, having an epic viewing of all three seasons of *The Borgias*! The sumptuous costumes, the luxurious palaces, the passion and murder and danger. Not to mention Cesare's eyes… I've always loved the Italian Renaissance, the beauty and intrigue of it. And I loved finding the characters of Isabella and her Orlando among the *palazzi* and riverbanks of Florence.

The pinnacle of danger in the Renaissance came with the famous Pazzi Conspiracy of 1478. It was an attempt by a few members of the ancient Pazzi family, along with some powerful allies including the pope, to displace Lorenzo de Medici as the *de facto* ruler of Florence. On April 26, 1478, they rose up in the midst of a crowd of ten thousand at Mass in the Duomo to assassinate Lorenzo and his handsome younger brother, Giuliano. Lorenzo escaped; Giuliano did not. The failure of the conspiracy led directly to a two-year war with the papacy that strengthened the power of Lorenzo.

I always love incorporating real historical figures into my fictional stories. Botticelli is one of my favourite artists. I once made a nuisance of myself standing way too long in front of his *Primavera*, taking in every detail. I was so happy to make him a friend of Isabella! Isabella's cousins Matteo and Caterina are not real, though Giuliano de Medici certainly might have been in love with the beautiful, fragile Caterina, who is loosely based on his real love, Simonetta Vespucci, who died young of tuberculosis and was the model for many of Botticelli's paintings. I think my Caterina, though, still has a tale to tell...and love of her own to find! Fiencosole, too, is a fictional town, but based on some of the many walled, beautiful fiefdoms of Renaissance Italy.

Some great sources I found useful in my research were:

CB Schmitt, ed, *The Cambridge History of Renaissance Philosophy* (1988)

Tim Parks, *Medici Money: Banking, Metaphysics, and Art in Fifteenth-Century Florence* (2005)

James Barter, *A Travel Guide to Renaissance Florence* (2003)

Lauro Martines, *April Blood: Florence and the Plot against the Medici* (2003)

Christopher Hibbert, *The House of Medici: Its Rise and Fall* (1974)

Pier Luigi De Vecchi and Daniel Arasse, *Botticelli: From Lorenzo the Magnificent to Savonarola* (2003)

I loved writing Isabella and Orlando's tale, and I hope you enjoy reading it! For more information on Renaissance Florence, be sure to visit my website at http://ammandamccabe.com.

MILLS & BOON®

Why shop at millsandboon.co.uk?

Each year, thousands of romance readers find their perfect read at millsandboon.co.uk. That's because we're passionate about bringing you the very best romantic fiction. Here are some of the advantages of shopping at www.millsandboon.co.uk:

* **Get new books first**—you'll be able to buy your favourite books one month before they hit the shops

* **Get exclusive discounts**—you'll also be able to buy our specially created monthly collections, with up to 50% off the RRP

* **Find your favourite authors**—latest news, interviews and new releases for all your favourite authors and series on our website, plus ideas for what to try next

* **Join in**—once you've bought your favourite books, don't forget to register with us to rate, review and join in the discussions

Visit **www.millsandboon.co.uk**
for all this and more today!